THE
DRIVE IN

DOUGLAS GARDHAM

THE DRIVE IN

iUniverse books may be ordered through booksellers or by contacting:

iUniverse
1663 Liberty Drive
Bloomington, IN 47403
www.iuniverse.com
1-800-Authors (1-800-288-4677)

ISBN: 978-1-4917-4814-5 (sc)
ISBN: 978-1-4917-4815-2 (e)

Printed in the United States of America.

iUniverse rev. date: 12/05/2014

THE
DRIVE IN

To Patricia and Rogers, my Mom and Dad,
for demonstrating and living the importance of family

*Most men lead lives of quiet desperation
and go to the grave with the song still in them.*
—Henry David Thoreau

Table of Contents

From Dusk 'til Dawn

The Trailer

Today was going to be different. He'd thought about it, reasoned it out, and was ready to make his pitch. They would hear him this time. He just knew they would. His prototype, his business plan—they all fit together. The idea was too important to miss again. The video of the remote model car he'd worked on for weeks proved the concept. The picture that lay ahead of them was magnificent. The board had to see the possibilities this time.

It was then he saw the lights—the bright strobes of an emergency vehicle flashing in his rearview mirror. His heart shot to his throat as it always did when the flash of police lights lit up his mirrors. *What did he do wrong?* was always the first thing to come to mind. His speedometer showed he was barely over the limit. A pair of red taillights lit up in front of him.

Two cars were ahead. One, like his, slowed at the side of the road. The other no longer looked like a car but a tangled mass of automotive carnage sitting just beyond a gouged-out section of neatly trimmed hedge that edged the side of the road he passed every day.

Tom's foot was on the brake pedal. All thought vanished outside of imagining what had gone so wrong only a few seconds earlier.

Tom wasn't aware he'd brought the BMW to a stop. Nor was he aware that he'd exited his car and was running, without having turned off his car.

It was incredible how much it looked like something he might have envisioned. The puddle under the front of the car—black and round—like any other puddle really. *It's not blood,* he thought. It might have been were it a movie. Yes, in fact, that's how it felt—like a movie set, surreal and staged, unreal. He didn't recognize the woman inside the crushed car. She was talking as he approached, pleading for help, looking at him like he'd been her best friend for years. The wreckage had occurred in mere seconds. The devastation would last his lifetime.

There was a gash across her forehead. Blood covered her left eye and streamed down the left side of her thin, pretty neck. She was holding a beautiful mauve scarf, one she'd likely put on staring back at her reflection in the floor-length mirror in the front foyer of her home, just before putting her arm in the sleeve of her no-longer-white waist jacket. Large, white buttons that drew attention to the front of her coat were done up almost to her slender neck and spotted with blood.

"Please help me," she begged, spitting as she spoke. Her right eye, as large as a baseball, stared back at him or at something. "I'm going to be late for work."

Tom reached forward, all but frozen by what he saw, and accepted her hand. He stared at it. The warm softness was alarming in the destruction around them. Her grip was light but firm.

The Lord is my shepherd ... began in his head.

"Tell Jenny ... it'll be okay ..."

The woman spoke in little more than a whisper. Seeing the brilliant crimson on the stark white of her jacket was like a stiff whiff of ammonia up his nose. The intensity of the moment was brought into slow motion, crystal clarity.

The woman's startling blue eye looked at him.

"Please tell Jenny ..." she whispered again.

Her lip quivered. Her grip tightened and then left him. Her eye stopped moving.

Mile Zero

Tom Johnson was wide-awake before his alarm went off. Between dreaming and opening his eyes, his mind was spinning, as often was the case when work was needling him. He couldn't seem to let it go. He was flipping between quitting to do something he wanted to do and staying to keep up the good fight. Tom always wanted to feel connected to his work. In the past, when he wasn't, he'd moved on to a new company. Recently, the atmosphere in the office had shifted, catching him with his gloves down and a left hook he never saw coming. One moment he was developing ideas for the company's new product—a control interface for industrial equipment—and the next, scratching his nearly bald head as to why he was even there. Business was booming. The economy was strong. The company was moving in yet another new direction—the third in as many months. There was more business to be had. The company's products needed something more, something to differentiate them. Terms like *ease of use*, *smart interfaces*, and *ergonomic design* were being batted about like baseballs in a batting cage, garnering lots of attention with little more reason than everybody else was using them. It was daily iteration and more than a little boring to Tom. Same old, same old. Different words for the same outcome he had seen time and time again. Hence his dilemma and sleeping discord.

When his alarm finally buzzed its five o'clock wake-up, his hand shot out from under the covers to shut it off. Janet, whom he'd woken up beside for almost ten years, didn't stir.

In the dark, he eased himself out from under the warm blankets. Like most days, he pulled the bed sheets up to his pillow, a habit carried over from childhood. To anyone watching, it might have looked like he was attempting to cover up having slept there. The hardwood they'd had installed throughout the house was cool to his bare feet, but he preferred the grip to wearing socks. He looked over at Janet in the dim light and wondered if she was happy. After Jill and Lacey were born, their intimacy suffered the most. Love had become a mixed array of feelings. His preference would have been to climb back under the blankets and hold her. He pressed his morning erection against his palm. To feel her hot skin against his would be heaven. It would allow him some escape from all that was on his mind. To have her naked breasts brush against his chest. To touch the lips he so longed to kiss and then make love to her. But at five in the morning it would only serve to piss her off. Instead of bringing them together, it would drive her further away. The girls took most of her energy these days, leaving little for him. As quietly as he could, he closed their bedroom door and crept downstairs to the basement.

Today didn't feel different than any other day. First was exercise. It was tough to get started, but once he did, he never stopped until he was done. Discipline—that unnatural of human attributes—got him there and kept him going.

Push-ups, sit-ups, chins, curls, squats, and more push-ups had his blood really pumping before thoughts of the meeting he had scheduled for later that day surfaced. His stomach turned over on itself. Tom had what he thought was the future staring back at him. Not just for the company but for the modern world. It was a very new idea for the company. What had become the toughest part of his job was convincing those he worked with to believe in something *he* saw as the future without the board's consent. Today's meeting had to be different. In his previous presentation, the board didn't get what he was talking about. The vice president of finance had shut him down. "Just stick to the program, Tom. Don't get creative. We need profitable products, not needless risk." But his idea continued to gain clarity despite contradicting the company mind-set he was supposed to be promoting to his group. *Sometimes you have to step out* kept whispering in his ear. On a good day, he was inspired to do so, but on others, he didn't have the energy. Trying to create something under the radar added stress to his already busy days. It churned his stomach and woke him before his alarm. He needed relief. Exercise helped.

Stretching killed him. It was the part of exercise that made him feel his forty-four years of age the most. His body seemed to age in inverse proportion to his brain. As his body deteriorated, his brain seemed to strengthen. Sitting on the floor with his left leg out straight in front of him, he bent forward. In years past, he could touch his straightened knee with his nose. But those days were gone. He could barely get his nose within six inches of his knee on a good day. As he stretched, he thought of his work. Software and the computer had given business so much flexibility. Yet like his body, as a business grew older and more established it became slower and more difficult to maneuver. Systems—the "brains" required to operate the business—became more complex to deal with the growth in data and processes. As processes became more ingrained and ever present, the company seemed more averse to change prohibiting new ideas to flourish. Like him, the company had become stiff and loathed stretching.

As usual, it took Tom thirty minutes to go through his routine.

Back upstairs to the main level with time ticking, he kept moving. After a bowl of Shreddies and a grapefruit, he bounded to the second floor, his feet light on the steps so as not to wake anyone.

Twenty minutes later, showered and dressed, he kissed Janet on the cheek and paused for a moment. Beautiful in sleep, he knew and loved her like no other. Time had changed things, but it wasn't just time. It was what he was doing with his time and how impossible it seemed to change the direction he was headed.

Into the garage via the laundry room, he opened the driver's door on his prized BMW and climbed in. If traffic was good, the odds were in his favor to be in the office shortly before seven.

For Tom Johnson, getting behind the wheel of his black BMW was second only to sex—and it never rejected him.

As the garage door opened, the BMW exited into the growing morning light. The car's headlights were on but of little use. He drove forward like Batman in the Batmobile out of the Batcave. A gust of wind blew into his windshield and shook the car. He was glad he wasn't walking and smiled at the creature comforts that surrounded him. Leaving the driveway, he pressed the garage door remote on the console and turned left onto the street.

His usual route was across Main, left at the lights and down Roosevelt. A quick right on French took him out to the two-lane Highway 6, but more importantly past Coffee Express and his morning reward. It was hard to beat that first sip of hot coffee with double cream. There was only one car ahead of him in the drive-through. He passed on the proffered donut even though he'd earned it. Then it was back out and onto the highway, or Pickens Run as some of the locals liked to call it. Way back during prohibition, Johnny Pickens liked to run his moonshine south to the city down this route. Little more than a two-rut pathway back then, the route didn't change, and the name stuck. Tom, in his black BMW, eons from the Model-T Fords of the time, made his way south down the long, five-mile stretch of highway to Dolan.

His mind soon became lost in the day ahead, but it wasn't work that had his attention. It was Silke that filled his thoughts, as often was the case once he'd left the comforts of his home. Silke was a member of his team but more to the point she was the woman he obsessed about sleeping with. From their first meeting, he knew he would have to be careful. She held a power that only a female can over a man. And he was vulnerable. Disciplined, yes, but still a man with eyes. Silke was irresistible. He'd assigned her an office up the hall from his to keep the picture of running his hands up her creamy smooth thighs at bay. She was a distraction. He was distractible.

It was anguish to think that making love to Janet had become her once-a-month act of duty as his wife—and his release. In between had become like that once read book that's placed on the shelf and rarely opened or even touched, yet filled with delight. The periods of absence drove him close to madness, looking for ways to adjust. He loved Janet, but the temptation of Silke and his curiosity were growing beyond his power to resist. Just thinking of Silke made things better and work more tolerable.

The BMW came up on the old farmhouse on the outskirts of Dolan that he drove past every day. There was nothing remarkable about the gray-white two-story. The second-floor window that faced the roadway, usually dark at this time, was lit this morning. Somebody was up early. He often wondered what went on behind the windows of this house. He had passed it for years but knew nothing of its occupants. *What were they doing different this morning for the light to be on?*

The Room for Rent sign he remembered passing on other mornings was gone.

Daphne heard a car pass outside her window. It was something she was having difficulty getting used to at her new location—all the passing cars and trucks. It woke her up early and made going back to sleep near impossible. Thank the good Lord for books. She loved the feel of books in her hands—especially new ones. The pages were crisp and fresh in her fingers. She couldn't wait to get started on *The Old Man and the Sea* to see what new world was awaiting her arrival? The words that filled the pages would help her settle into her new community.

Feature No. 1—*The Gift*

Rain pelted the roof of the East Queen streetcar as an early-morning storm raged across the city. It was Friday—and the fifth straight morning of rain. Gloom permeated everything, including Daphne's mood. Only the paperback she held in her lap and the occasional snippet of overheard conversation of other passengers offered her any reprieve from the lousy weather.

Long, strawberry-blonde hair fell to her shoulders. On first acquaintance, most would say she was shy and withdrawn. But having been raised on early-morning chores and hard work, there was strength behind that shyness. She was a country girl in a big city, out of her element but adjusting. It was hard, but not near what admitting defeat would be in returning to the farm. She faced the front of the streetcar, her left arm against the cool metal side. Her knapsack was between her feet.

She stared at the page in her book, not reading the words but thinking of the day ahead. Normally, in twenty minutes, she would be at her desk at Davis and Sloan, preparing to field the myriad of customer complaints she had to respond to every day. She thought of her boss, Mr. Robinson, who would not be at work today. Of the bulging eyes that ogled her breasts before uttering a simple "good morning"; a mangy dog received more respect.

Why had she come to Toronto anyway?

She didn't like to think about the answer to that question. But she wasn't going back. Not now. Not ever.

The words from her book came into focus.

"I've had enough," spoke the heroine. "Today will be different."

Daphne smiled. Today *would* be different.

The streetcar jerked to a stop. A man and woman stepped on. Daphne paid no attention until the woman took the seat beside her. *Why did she have to sit there?* There were other seats. It made her uncomfortable. She didn't like people in her space, never mind a stranger. The smell of lilacs filled the air.

"Good morning," said the woman before Daphne could turn back to her book.

Daphne forced a smile but remained silent. She didn't talk to people she didn't know, especially those on buses in Toronto. People who did had problems. She had enough of her own. One never knew what lay behind the words of a stranger. Besides, to suggest it was anything close to a *good* morning was ludicrous. Was the woman blind?

"Great day to be alive," the woman stated her voice bright. Daphne wondered where the sun was that this woman was seeing.

Again she smiled, as was her custom when confronted with comments she had no idea how to reply to. She was not in the mood for a chatty Cathy.

Daphne looked back at the page in her book, doing her best to ignore the woman.

Strange, Daphne thought. Despite the gloom clinging to everything else, the woman seemed happy. Sunshine appeared to radiate from the woman's face. She was big-boned with heavy, fat thighs that pressed against Daphne's. The contact was all but unbearable. For the woman to evaporate would have suited Daphne just fine. Dark eyebrows met above the woman's thick, Roman nose. Her eyes were too close together to be pretty. Long, auburn hair—her best feature—flowed down her back. Shiny and clean, she'd likely washed and styled it before the break of dawn. Her sleeveless summer dress, patterned with large, yellow flowers, exacerbated rather than slimmed her flabby arms. Men wouldn't give the woman a second glance, but that wouldn't have bothered this woman in the least.

"I'm so lucky," she said, turning toward Daphne. "He's finally gone."

Daphne made no effort to reply, assuming the woman was missing not only a few spades but diamonds and clubs as well. Back on the farm, Daphne had known people like her. Back home, twisted Henny Blackwood, who carried a teddy bear like most women carried a purse, would approach anyone on the street and natter away about some piece of nonsense. "The woman's hair went all curly white seeing that dead husband of hers in the bathtub." Everyone knew the crazy kook and what they were in for if she caught up with them. Toronto had its fill of these social pariahs who came in a variety of packages. She saw them on street corners and at bus stops. She was not about to pay this woman any more attention and refocused on the page of her paperback and the knapsack at her feet.

"Told him many times, I did," the woman kept up, smoothing the floral print on her dress across her lap with thick-fingered hands. "But no, he wouldn't listen. Too smart for that, he was."

The woman stopped, but Daphne knew more was coming.

"You know. He had it good—*real* good. I gave him everything. And he loved me for it, you know. Told me so. He'd smile sometimes. Like only a man smiles at a woman. Like he's on top of the world. Know what I mean?"

Daphne knew the smile, knew it well. It was a smile of power, a smile of control and conquest. When men smiled like that at her, it was not the top of the world they were thinking about. The men she had been with wanted one thing and one thing only. Sex. They wanted to fuck. She'd run away from the farm to escape it. But it didn't matter where she went. It was everywhere. Just like the bastard she'd worked for. It was a smile that meant one thing—beware.

"Only men smile that way. You know, they get plugged in or something." Again, the woman stopped. She raised her hand and touched her cheek.

"Then everything changed," she said. The woman's voice grew louder as she turned toward Daphne and continued, "He never smiled no more. He got away on me." The woman leaned in close as if Daphne was a confidante and spoke just above a whisper. "I think it was his work."

Daphne didn't say a word. Staring at the page in front of her, she wanted to be somewhere else. But it wasn't her book that carried her away.

Instead, her thoughts drifted to her boss, Mr. Robinson. Big, thick, sweaty like a hog in a pen on a humid summer day Mr. Robinson. It made her think of slop and muck and shit-covered rubber boots. Her throat dried up. Her skin went prickly. It was her twelfth birthday. She was brushing Princess, her new pony, behind the barn. No one else was around. The friendly hired hand everyone liked said he would kill her momma if she opened the "'ole in her face." He smiled—a smile that could melt butter and just as quickly crack bones. It hurt. She remembered the straw poking into her face and having to lie to her momma about where the tiny cuts had come from. "Silly girl," her mother had said as if she'd slipped on a cow patty and fallen on her face. There was sharp pain as something hard and human was shoved up inside her, like sitting on a bike with no seat. She wasn't supposed to even stick her fingers up there. The utter loneliness that followed was worse: sitting on a hay bale with straw sticking into her bare bottom with no one to go to. She became detached from people, no longer able to talk to those she so needed. She wanted to die. She never told a soul. It wasn't the only time.

In high school, doing all she could to keep the lid on, she experienced another episode. Consent by trickery was the difference. She'd never forgiven herself for the indiscretion. Craving the closeness of another human being—such a fool—she was duped into an upstairs bedroom of a house she didn't know by the school's all-star quarterback. No one heard a thing. She never made a peep. She knew what was coming. Different but like before. There was no—and could never be—any justice. What was done was done. The police chief's son would never commit such a crime. She'd hear chants of "you little liar" if she'd made anything of it. Like before, silence was her guide. She did nothing. Hate and disgust were pent-up inside her. She was a bet, he'd told her with pride as he pumped his load into her bottom. It had nothing to do with human closeness where feelings were supposed to be mutual. He didn't lose, he said. It was all about control—about power.

Now with Mr. Robinson, it was all about power too, dick power. He had it, she didn't: his over hers.

He'd hired her on the spot. She'd started the same day.

She was excited at first—finally a man who had something more on his mind than screwing. He took interest in her work. Treated her like an equal. Talked to her and coached her on how she could improve her work. Told her how good a fit she was for the company. It was unbelievable, as unbelievable things usually are. She remembered being surprised when the first blip popped onto her radar. His hand had brushed against her arm when pulling a file from the cabinet beside her. It was brief, ever so light, but it was a touch. She didn't want to believe that it lingered. *It was instant*, she told herself, *only a moment*. But he had lingered, his skin on hers. Further to that, she wondered why he was even pulling a file when he could have simply asked her for it. Ever hopeful, she didn't want to believe it, so she didn't. She wouldn't admit there was something wrong, so proud of finding work in the big city by herself.

But after that first incident, his game was on.

His tactics were subtle and sophisticated. The next play came two days later, brushing against her while she retrieved a file from the cabinets in the narrow alcove adjacent to her desk. Once was accidental, but twice was unmistakable. How many times would she deny herself into false belief? Occurrences began to happen daily. How could she be so stupid—so ignorant? Handing him a cup of coffee, the morning newspaper, or a sandwich on a paper plate. Anytime their hands had occasion to touch, his would linger. It was as if long, penetrating tentacles would stretch from his fingers and invade her person. He would stand close to her while she took dictation. It's one thing to be fooled, but fooling herself broke something inside her, something she refused to break again.

Mr. Robinson wanted the same things the others did—he was just more cunning in his approach. There was something in his head—evil was her word for it—that somehow made it part of her work. It incensed her to have not recognized his ploy from the beginning.

But a job was a job. She had rent to pay and food to buy. Besides, she was in familiar territory. She could handle it. In a manner befitting a country girl supposedly naïve to the world's ways, she ignored his advances. But nothing changed. It never did. The frequency of his come-ons simply varied. He would indicate disinterest and then come back with renewed vigor. In the past, the only effective way to end things was to get away from the bastards. But here, she needed the job and was afraid if she lost this one she might never find another.

He'd asked her to stay late—a serious deadline was pending. He'd asked before without success. She had things to do. But this time, there was a hundred dollars in it for her.

"I lived with him for twelve years, I did," Daphne heard the woman say, disrupting Daphne's recollection. "You'd think a person in their rightful mind would do something about it, wouldin'cha?"

Daphne smiled and nodded.

You'd think so, wouldin'cha, Daphne?

The streetcar slowed for a red light. The rain continued its relentless drumming on the metal roof. Rainwater streamed down the windows in heavy rivulets that distorted the view outside.

"I'm such an idiot," the woman continued as if the two of them were friends sitting down to a cup of coffee. "I should've seen it coming."

The woman's voice sunk into Daphne's thoughts. Despite having her book still open on her lap, the story was gone. Her fingertips pressed hard into the page she was on.

Men did not leave her alone. They wanted a piece of "Daff." She stared at her broken thumbnail. A flurry of blurred images rushed through her head.

File folders. An electric saw. Green garbage bags.

They all had it coming. He got what he deserved.

"No note. Nothing. He just never came home," the woman said. Daphne hardly heard her. She was reliving the night before.

He knew she needed the money. There was always work to do in the gray office. It was all too easy. Knowing what would follow, she agreed to stay. A hundred bucks was too much to pass up. She could handle it.

At first he left her alone typing his handwritten notes into the computer. But on opening the third file, she heard the metal scrape of a drawer sliding open from the filing cabinets behind her. He had waited long enough and was on his prowl.

"Where's the Jacobsen file?" rang his loud, high-pitched voice, startling her from behind.

"It's in the black cabinet at the back," she answered. "Top drawer."

Daphne returned to her typing, listening as he made his way toward the front of the office and her desk, ignoring her answer. His footfalls stopped. Close by, another filing cabinet scraped open. Her eyes shifted from the computer screen. Anticipating his next move, she waited. More metal scraping broke the quiet as he pulled yet another steel drawer open.

The screeching brakes of the streetcar returned her to her seat beside the fat woman. The streetcar stopped.

"Not even a phone call," she heard the woman say. "I phoned his office, ya know ..."

Daphne didn't hear the rest. Instead came the sound of his wheezing close behind her.

"No, it's not," he announced. "It's right here. Somebody's being a bad girl."

She cringed at his raised voice and rose from her chair, certain of what would follow. His subtle come-ons were one thing, but this was something new. The file *was* at the back. He'd found it and now wanted her to role-play some kind of *bad girl* scenario.

"Mr. Robinson, I know the file was in the cabinet at the back," she said, needing to stop him before he got going any further. At the same time, something clicked inside her head like a stopwatch—time was up.

For as long as she could remember, men had a need to touch her, to use her, to fuck her—especially older men.

He had liked to touch her budding breasts at night when *he* tucked her into bed. At first it seemed inadvertent. *He* would apologize. Then later, *he* told her it was okay. *He* was her daddy. All daddies loved their daughters, except *he* was not her daddy. *He* was her mother's boyfriend, her mother's man about the house. Worst of all, her mother knew and did nothing about it.

The letter opener was in the top drawer of her desk. She moved sideways and eased the drawer open. Her hand found the thin strip of stainless steel. Dutifully she left her desk and walked toward Mr. Robinson, slipping the weapon into the pocket of her black slacks.

"In some ways it's a miracle," said the woman, interrupting Daphne's memory and then just as quickly fading out again.

The wall of filing cabinets was on her right. He stood at the end holding the yellow file folder in his hand.

"It was in the back cabinet this morning, Mr. Robinson," she said in her most pleasant calm voice. "I put it there."

"Well it's not there now!" he sneered. "It was right here."

He patted the front of the open drawer level with his belly.

Stepping forward, she shoved the drawer into the cabinet as hard as she could. As she did, his hand touched her blonde head. Her blood iced. As she turned, his hand lingered, brushing against her shoulder. Her right hand slid into her pocket, her fingers wrapping around the pointed metal opener. With her other hand, she touched his arm.

"That's better," he said as his hand came around to the center of her back. Her teeth clenched, holding back the nausea that curdled in her stomach.

Her left hand moved across the white, wrinkled, cotton-polyester material that stretched across his bulging gut, fully focused on pulling the silver weapon out of her pocket.

"Come on, baby," he said, shoving her against the front of the cabinets. Both of her elbows banged the metal fronts, her right hand still in her back pocket. She tried to resist him, but his bulk easily overpowered her as he pressed himself against her.

"You want this as much as I do," he hissed in her ear, his hand squeezing her breast. "I'm gonna give you what you want, baby."

His hands became a fury of activity across her chest, mashing her breasts and ripping her sweater. A button fell to the floor.

His sweaty face pressed against hers. The sickening smell of mustard and onions engulfed her as his open mouth attacked her tight lips.

"Come on, babe. You know you want it."

He ripped open the front of her white blouse as her fingers touched the metal in her pocket. Her sweater slid from her shoulders and would handcuff her if forced any further down her arms. His rough hands pinched her, reddening her pale skin as her hand came away with the weapon. The ease with which he shoved her against the filing cabinets reinforced the fear he held over her. Despite his flab, his strength was daunting.

As if suddenly mindful of what she intended to do, she lost her grip on the opener. It fell to the floor.

"Not even a note," said the woman beside her. Daphne flipped the paperback over on her lap and pressed her palm down on the spine. She squeezed her knee with her other hand. The woman shook. "I wanted him to leave, but …"

His face was like sandpaper against the side of her soft cheek. He was a wild dog trying to fuck a stray bitch—just low, raw, animal. Daphne clutched the left leg of her slacks. His hands were at her waist, struggling with the button on the front. He slid down her body, groping her thighs, totally oblivious to anything around him.

"Show me what you got, Daff," he growled as he pulled her pants down over her hips. His face mashed into her groin. "You smell like you need it."

"He wasn't a bad man. Not mean in that sense," the woman said, her words incongruent with Daphne's memory. "But still …"

Still what? Daphne asked herself, feeling his presence close by.

"You know what I mean. They all gotta get off. It's like they'll explode or something."

Daphne stared in horror at the letter opener on the floor. As he pulled her pants down to her ankles, his hand came close to her weapon. With his face in her crotch, she watched his hand slide even closer. She closed her eyes and lifted her head, knowing it was over.

In the same instant, something else came to her, and her hands went to his greasy, bald head. She didn't feel anything but his sliminess on her hands and thighs. Like shoving her hands into excrement, she pushed his head into her. With her back against the cabinets, she then slid down until her face was in front of his. She would play his game once.

Forcing her face into his, she managed the unthinkable and ground her lips into his. The coppery taste of blood entered her mouth. He responded as anticipated, engulfed by his own corrupt lust and power.

"Oh my god," he uttered.

With raging hate, she snatched up the steel and stood up. Keeping force on his head with her left hand, she held him against her. He licked her like a sick dog licks a wound.

Her arm was in the air with the top of his bald head at her belly. Thought left her.

Her tight right fist came down in one swift motion.

Time vanished.

Daphne held a death grip on the handle of the letter opener. One moment he was on her like a rabid animal. The next, he was sliding to the floor, pulling her down with an imbecilic look of disbelief in his eyes. She let go and stared at the silver handle sticking from the side of his head.

"There's days I should have killed him," said the plump woman. Daphne heard the words but could not connect them with anything in her mind. She tried to focus on what the woman said, forcing the nightmare from her thoughts. "But I could never bring myself to do such a thing. I …"

The streetcar shuddered to another stop. A man in a suit stepped aboard. Perspiration broke out across Daphne's forehead.

"He always interrupted me. Never listened. Didn't care what I said. Even hit me on occasion. That's when I says …"

Emotion left the woman's voice. She spoke as if reading the words from the front page of the *Toronto Star*.

"At first it was jabs in my stomach. 'You're empty,' he says to me." Crossing her arms, she grabbed her shoulders as if chilled by a cool breeze.

"He broke my wrist once," she said, clenching her left hand in front of Daphne, indicating the injury. "I was washing the kitchen floor. I was in his way. His beer was in the fridge."

Daphne caught herself staring wide-eyed at the woman, in disbelief.

She fought the urge to speak. The heroine in her book had her arm slashed for holding out on her pimp. Men were like that.

15

Boyfriends, husbands, and one-night stands—they were all the same. Most thought they had a right to do whatever they wanted to their women—pride of ownership.

Mr. Robinson did not say a word. His arms and hands flailed uselessly at his sides in a macabre floor dance. None of it seemed real. His lips curled grotesquely into a twisted S shape. His eyes, wide and white, finally locked on a spot on the ceiling. He became still. There was little blood.

"You know I did try once," the woman said, bringing Daphne back yet again to the streetcar. "To kill him, I mean."

Daphne turned in amazement from the wet grayness outside to face the woman.

"I poured cooking oil on the basement steps one night," said the woman in a lowered voice, sharing a confidence. "Greased them up good. Then I asked him to get me something from the freezer downstairs."

Daphne heard the woman's words but could not get the image of his still body out of her mind.

Frozen in fright, she stood looking down at him, unsure of what to do next. Blood drooled from the wound around the blade stuck in his greasy bald head. Without thinking, she pulled out the letter opener. Why she did, she wasn't sure, but blood immediately gushed onto her hand and across the floor. She grabbed the wastebasket beside the filing cabinets and slid it over his head. What followed was a mixture of confusion and the practice of animal slaughter.

His corpse was too heavy for her to move alone. He outweighed her by a hundred pounds or more. But she couldn't leave him on the floor. The police would take little time to find her out. The courts would never understand. To be charged with murdering the bastard would exceed all injustice in the world. It wasn't going to happen on her watch. Simply, she had to figure out a way to get rid of the body.

There wasn't time to think it all through. She ran to her desk to no avail. She crossed the hall to the washroom, her blue eyes darting everywhere. Panic pumped adrenaline through her veins as she clung to self-control, forcing herself to concentrate. Near her wit's end and broaching thoughts that flight might be her best option, she thought of the janitor's closet. In seconds, she was down the hall, yanking open the door, and crashing into a mop and bucket. Her heart sank as her eyes scanned the shelves filled with cleaning agents, paper towels, and plastic bags, seeing nothing of use. She was about to give up when her arm brushed against a black electric cord hanging down from an upper shelf. The cord was attached to an electric jigsaw. She'd never seen it used in the office but knew what it was from working in the shed back home. Intended for wood, it worked magic on animal bones. Her plan became clear.

In seconds she was back beside the body, saw in hand. It was impossible to believe what she was about to embark on. She'd helped haul dead animals around the farm—even watched their slaughter— but never anything like this.

"But it didn't work," the woman said, shaking her head as Daphne was pulled back to the present. "He just swore at me for being stupid."

Daphne looked out the window, unable to quit her memory.

After a moment's hesitation, she plugged in the saw. Like the cows and pigs she had seen butchered as a girl, she remembered how the blood and guts had covered everything. She ran back to the janitor's closet and grabbed a box of green garbage bags. She ripped open half a dozen and spread them out on the brown carpet beside his corpse. With effort, she rolled the body onto the shiny plastic, taking care to keep the head inside the wastebasket. She could not bear to look at the face nor afford the spill of any more blood.

"Gone ... never came home last night," the woman said. "Haven't heard a word."

The loud buzz of the electric saw broke the silence around her. She jumped. Her finger slipped off the trigger. It took a moment for her to refocus and start again.

The first cut was the worst. Starting with the lower left leg, the blade sliced through the fleshy calf like she was cutting raw prime rib. It was surprisingly smooth until the blade caught the bone. She held tight and pushed hard. The saw was the ticket.

After removing the foot, she realized she had to contain the body pieces in some manner. In the small kitchen, she found a box of large

Ziploc bags. She cut each body piece to size, slipped it in a bag, and sealed it. She worked feverishly. Blood ran everywhere. Fortunately the blade was sharp and, other than a few snags on bone and muscle, cut like a knife through warm Brie. After two hours and six green garbage bags, she was done. The head remained in the wastebasket.

The bags spread across the floor worked well to contain the gooey gore. She mopped up the mess of blood and foul body fluid, emptying what she could down the office toilet. What remained, including the mop head, went in a garbage bag.

"You know I can't believe it," Daphne heard the woman say, returning her to the streetcar. "He worked so hard."

Yeah, I'll bet he did, Daphne thought.

Standing in the hallway opposite the filing cabinets, she had to think of a way to get rid of the bags. How, in the middle of the night in this big city, could she possibly make two hundred pounds of human disappear?

Incineration or a big bonfire would do the trick back on the farm, but there was no time for that. Landfill was the only answer. She doubled up and repacked each bag with newspaper and other garbage to hide, as best she could, the meaty feel of what lie inside. Two cans of Lysol from the janitor's closet helped hide the growing odor she began to detect. Not as noticeable to her olfactory senses, city folk were sure to notice the unsavory smell. She then called a taxi and carried the green bags to the street, one bag at a time. The last bag contained the contents of the wastebasket. She decided to stuff it in her knapsack for no other reason than feeling it might be put to better use later. She locked up and met the taxi out front.

After the last bag was loaded in the trunk, she told the heavyset, bearded driver to head to the closest landfill. If luck were part of her picture in any way, Mr. Robinson's wallet had three hundred dollars in it. She handed the driver two hundred and told him he'd never seen her.

He nodded and didn't say a word.

Fifteen minutes later, they were unloading the bags at a twenty-four-hour dumpsite in the east end.

"Works at Davis and Sloan," the woman explained, her voice trailing off as she turned her head. "He's the boss. I'm going there now."

Daphne froze, realizing she knew the woman beside her—or at least had heard enough about the woman to know her. Her hand pressed down even harder on her book. Her calves squeezed against the knapsack at her feet.

"What do you think my chances are?" the woman asked. Daphne turned and faced the woman.

"For what?" she asked, her voice hard and on edge. It was the first time she'd spoken.

"Of getting him back of course," the woman replied as if it were a simple matter of fact.

Daphne's eyes grew wide in astonishment.

The streetcar stopped. They were two stops before the Davis and Sloan exit. But Daphne was not going to work—not today.

"Excuse me, ma'am," she said as she stood up. The woman moved to let her pass.

She picked up her knapsack. She had intended to toss it into Lake Ontario after collecting a couple of large rocks. But a better plan now occurred to her.

"Here," she said, proffering the knapsack to the woman. "Call it my gift to you. You need it more than I do."

She left the knapsack on the seat. As she stepped off the streetcar, she flipped a quick glance at the woman she had bestowed the special gift upon. It was time to move on.

The streetcar's heavy steel wheels pounded their engagement into the steel track. Daphne began her anonymous walk westward along Queen Street East in the rain.

As she walked, she listened. A horn sounded. A car tire splashed through puddles on the street. A bell jingled on a door front. A brightness came upon her she had not noticed before. She had not gone far when she stopped. Listening, she was certain she heard it. It was distant and faint like the steel-on-steel shriek of the streetcar's wheels against the rails—or a woman's scream.

Mile Seven

Tom rounded the curve out of Dolan, already having forgotten the old farmhouse with the gray-white siding and the lit second-floor window. He was trying to focus on others things—more important things—as he straightened out the BMW.

He sipped his coffee.

The radio was on with the news. The female announcer spoke about the victim of a homicide "… reported last week was identified as a Mr. James Robinson whose dismembered body parts were found in a knapsack on Queen Street …"

Tom reached for the dial and turned off the radio. He didn't need disturbing news fouling his day. There was enough of that already. But it did make him think of death—that final frontier of humanity.

What would he do if he knew he couldn't fail? Sure as shit, he wasn't doing it these days.

He drove up the hill sided by Pine Hills Golf and Country Club. The sun had just about cleared the horizon. The golf course staff was into its early morning routine of preparing the course for the day's golfers. Tom, though, wasn't thinking of the new Callaways hanging in his garage. Instead, it was the greens keepers crossing the fairways on their mowers beside their long morning shadows. They weren't worried about corporate direction or misdirected ideals. There was no made-up work. It was about cutting grass—nature's garden—and keeping it properly groomed.

Once past the golf course, he was en route to Riverview and the familiar bungalow on the outskirts. The house caused Tom to reflect for the thousandth time on whether he should move the family closer to his work. Riverview wasn't that much closer but he liked the house. It had character—at least from what he could see from the road with its high peaked roof and columned entrance. But he always came to the same conclusion—it really wouldn't shorten his drive much, it would be hard on Jill and Lacey, and it was all but impossible to justify.

He kept driving and reached for his coffee. A sip always made things a little more bearable.

Despite the giant advances in technology shrinking the globe, the workplace continued to be in or close to the large urban centers. For many like Tom, living there was beyond their means, so commuting from suburbia was a way of life.

His thoughts turned to his driverless car idea. The commute would cease to matter with a driverless vehicle, as the time behind the wheel could be replaced by doing something more valuable than driving. People could live anywhere. There was no doubt driverless cars *were* the future.

Tom knew he had reached the point where he couldn't let it go. Driverlessness—a word not in any dictionary yet—was coming and more than a little obvious. But any time he spoke the word in the presence of others, chuckles were sure to follow.

"A car driven by itself," one executive said, smiling. "Are you serious Tom? It'll never be."

Another youthful engineer quipped, "You ever seen *The Fast and the Furious*? Not gonna happen."

Tom's response, that he usually kept to himself, was always the same—*until it does.*

Driverlessness had become part of Tom's vocabulary. He was trying to make it part of the company's. No, they didn't manufacture cars, but they knew interfaces and controls like nobody else. Tom saw it like the Microsoft-IBM collaboration of years past. The computer needed an interface, an operating system like DOS, to give it directions. A driverless car would need the same thing. Tom was convinced the car would become the computer that moved people around. It would need its own operating system. Why not them?

But daily, he was jerked back to the reluctant, risk-adverse world of corporate business.

"An opportunity lies in front of us like no other," stated their CEO at a recent meeting Tom had attended. They could make their interface easier to use. It already was smart. They could make the box more ergonomic by rounding the edges. They would leap ahead of their competition. It was a no brainer. The market potential was enormous. They must take advantage of the opportunity.

Tom knew the controls world like the veins that crossed the back of his hand. There was little in the design of interfaces for industrial machinery he hadn't been exposed to since graduating from college. The difference this time around was his lack of enthusiasm for what the board wanted to do. They didn't see what he was talking about. They saw only the dollars their all-too-familiar interfaces commanded in the industrial equipment world. There was no room for risk, especially in a market they didn't know. Their customers knew what they wanted. Why mess with a good thing? "Our goal is growth" had become the company's motto. They had shareholders to please.

Add proportional control, update the screens with new symbols, maybe even a new box. "How about plastic?" one board member suggested. "Makes it lighter and *cool*," he said, expressing "cool" like the word itself was a new product.

Cost reduction was the name of the game. "Our new innovations help justify our premium price. Supply chain must work on cost. Five percent across the board." This was CEO-speak to motivate the company forward and had become Tom and team's primary responsibility.

But Tom wasn't about to give in. Driverlessness was too big a deal in his mind. He was convinced a driverless car was the future. Imagine not needing a driver to get around; a car that drove itself and took you wherever you wanted whenever you wanted. The possibilities were out of this world.

Coming up on the bungalow in Riverview, his driverless car replaced any thoughts of moving. A smile curved his lips. He still liked the house. It just didn't make any sense.

A For Sale sign was posted out near the highway. It had been there for months.

———◆———

He didn't much like the house anymore—too much stuff in the shadows. This was supposed to be their house—his and Cindy's. But that was not to be. It probably never was from the beginning. Cindy didn't like discussing it. "It's your parents' home. We can't live there." John knew better than to press the idea any further.

Cindy was right, of course, as often was the case. They couldn't live there. There were too many ghosts. His father had died almost four years ago, his mother a year later. He was their only child. The house was left to him. It'd been empty for a year.

The For Sale sign was up. Had been for a while. His real estate agent said the asking price was too high for the area, but John was determined, like he was with most everything in his life.

Feature No. 2—*Life in Love and Death*

"I'm here."

The words sounded louder in the empty foyer than he'd intended. He pushed the apartment door closed behind him. It seemed to have rained for days, and today was no different. His white cotton dress shirt was damp on his back. His overcoat was in the car. He couldn't be bothered with the damn thing.

"Another long day?" came a now familiar voice from behind the blank white wall in front of him.

He wiped his shoes on the mat and walked into her living room. It was furnished with a black leather couch and matching chair. Her minimalist décor was so different from the assortment of furnishings in every open spot of *their* apartment. The white walls were bare except for a small Picasso print above the couch. The only light came from a chrome floor lamp positioned beside the chair.

"Yes," he replied, his voice taking on a low, somber tone he hoped would prevent the need for an explanation.

"Pasta's almost ready."

"I need a drink."

He hadn't eaten all day but wasn't hungry. Like talk, food was unnecessary.

John crossed the living room to the area that served as her kitchen. Lauren was preparing dinner.

"Did they let you stay with her?"

"Yes."

In the small Hollywood kitchen, he pulled open one of the ivory-handled cupboard doors. Steam rose around Lauren as she stirred the contents of the copper pot at the stove. He pictured a woman vanishing as part of a magician's trick and thought of the life he now watched evaporate each day at the hospital. Something tightened in his stomach, something elastic and hard. He grabbed the brown bottle of Canadian Club on the shelf, seeking its warm comfort. Alcohol did ease enduring sorrow.

"Any improvement?"

"No," he uttered. "Nothing."

He unscrewed the gold plastic cap, having broken the seal the night before. He raised the bottle to his lips, anxious for the burn of the golden liquid. Instead he saw Cindy's beautiful brown eyes looking into his from her gaunt face—the ravages of the cancer. Had he no pride? He lowered the bottle and looked for a glass.

"Did she speak?"

"Yes."

He turned to face Lauren.

A forced smile creased her face. Tears were close. Her eyes were dark and heavy. He hated how she agonized over his feelings. She knew his pain. John knew only Cindy's. It was real and all but unbearable. Cindy was strong, but he'd had no idea of her strength. She fought with the courage of a thousand soldiers. Lauren's emotion sometimes got the best of her. These were difficult times for them both.

"She's dying ..."

He stopped, his voice quivering. Lauren knew the words, the feelings. He didn't want to cry any more, but his eyes swelled with tears.

He turned and poured the remainder of the bottle into the glass. He couldn't remember driving to Lauren's apartment from the hospital. For short periods, he could focus on what he saw, but most of the time his thoughts were elsewhere. Everything suffered—his work, his body, his mind. Life had become a minute-to-minute exercise of mind over matter and emotion control.

"Have you slept?" Lauren asked, looking into the pot of pasta.

"Not really."

Lauren continued stirring. Only the slosh of water in the pot was audible. John leaned back against the counter and gulped down his drink—a teaser. He waited for the burn. It wasn't near enough.

He crossed the parquet floor and sat down at the table. The kitchen space was small, little more than an alcove really. Lauren's husband had left her financially comfortable, but she lived like a pauper. The table was designed to swing into the wall, where it remained on most of his visits. Today, Lauren had readied the table for dinner.

John wanted to get drunk and talk about atoms and turtle shells and microbes, something that didn't matter. He didn't have the energy for hurt and feelings. Exhaustion was a blessing.

Lauren lifted the pot of pasta to the sink. The steam enveloped her, making the disappearance act all but complete while draining the noodles into a copper colander. Cindy had prepared pasta in much the same way—now only a memory from another time. Everyday activities he'd never thought much about and taken so for granted.

"What was that?" Lauren asked, raising her voice above the rush of water in the sink.

"Nothing," he answered, realizing he'd spoken his thoughts aloud. "It doesn't matter."

He stared at his emptied glass on the table.

A year ago, Cindy had been a healthy, vivacious, twenty-seven-year-old and his wife for four years. To John, she was everything—his best friend, his lover, and his muse. Like the cliché, love at first sight, it was when he first set eyes on her auburn head in their high school cafeteria a lifetime ago. Her long, slender legs and deep brown eyes wouldn't let him rest. She was never far from his thoughts. As seniors, they were inseparable. They hung out, went to movies, listened to jazz, and made love in between. Life was perfect.

After high school, they attended the University of Toronto—John in engineering, Cindy in fine arts. They married a month after graduation. They both found work in the city—John with a consulting firm, Cindy in graphic arts.

Life was wonderful; their pursuit of happiness attained.

After three years—hard to believe it was only a year ago—they decided to start a family. They wanted what they had spent years avoiding—for Cindy to get pregnant.

Cindy's cycle was like clockwork. She could predict it to the day. John could too—but he didn't need to count. Her mood swing was telltale enough. Unfortunately, their argument was usually over before it occurred to him.

After their third month of trying, it happened.

"John, I'm at five weeks—no blood!" Cindy had screamed she was so excited.

"Have you booked something with Dr. Dahar?"

"You better believe I have," she cried, swinging her arms around his neck.

A day later, she was suffering from severe abdominal cramps.

"John," she groaned, clenching her teeth against the pain, "I can't fucking stand it."

"Maybe I should take you to the ER?" he questioned.

Cindy shook her head at him. She could take it. "Its just part of it."

It was John's first inkling that something was wrong.

A day later, the morning of her doctor's appointment, he rushed her to the hospital. The pain was more than she could bear. Cindy couldn't stand upright.

That was a Monday—the last day of their normal life together.

Tuesday afternoon, Cindy was diagnosed with cancer of the uterus.

"I'm sorry," Dr. Dahar said, his face a solemn flatness as he looked first at John and then Cindy.

There was no baby.

The news was devastating. Cindy seemed more upset about the pregnancy than the cancer. John was scared to death. Cindy was his whole world. Tears had rolled down their shocked faces for hours. The doctor prescribed medication for her pain and sent them home. She was reexamined the following day and started chemo soon after.

John was numb for weeks. He walked around in a haze as if looking at the world through misted glasses. He withdrew into himself and found it difficult not only to speak to his sick wife but to even touch her. People no longer mattered. It was as if he was the one diagnosed with the disease. He talked little or not at all. Concentration was hopeless. They traveled to her medical appointments in silence, only speaking to the superfluous. He found it difficult to look at her, into those puppy-brown eyes, helpless to protect her from the insidious evil that attacked her body.

At first he found the thought absurd—how he'd not protected her from the disease—but that did little to ease his burden. In bouts of self-deprecating misery, he'd claim responsibility for her illness. What had he done to inflict such wickedness upon her? It was hard, so hard, to accept.

Many nights he would lie awake, listening to her slow, uneven breathing as she passed through dreams he would never share. He wanted to touch her soft, freckled shoulders, her smooth, slender neck but couldn't. He didn't want to wake her, but it went deeper than that. On seeing the spots of missing red hair, he would stop, frozen by the sight, unable to move, angered by his inability to kill the killer inside her.

He was certain she hated him: his inadequacy so prominent in her most vulnerable moment. "For better or worse," words he had promised only three short years before, seemed all but impossible to live up to.

And then something shifted his world.

He had taken Cindy to Princess Margaret Hospital for what had become her routine biweekly examination. While waiting, he browsed a dog-eared copy of *Architectural Digest*. A woman sat down beside him. He ignored her and was discomfited by her proximity. He shifted in his seat and stared at a dream house he would never share with Cindy when the woman spoke.

"It's not fair," she said, her voice trembling, holding back tears. "He's a good man."

John turned. At once, he was drawn both to the unknown woman and the need to comfort her. Tears ran down her flushed cheeks.

His eyes welled up in response. Embarrassed, he rubbed his forehead with his fingers to hide his unexpected reaction.

"I'm sorry," the woman said. "I didn't mean to upset you. It's just ..."

Lauren finished the sentence a month later over a deli sandwich at Colby's, a block from the hospital. Pancreatic cancer withered her husband to the grave four weeks later.

After Cindy's initial diagnosis, they rarely cried in front of each other. In their attempts to be strong, they shut each other off. Yet here he was relating to someone he had never met. Someone he needed that defied explanation.

John could not articulate his feelings for this woman. Simply put, she enabled him to talk. He held nothing from her. They talked about architecture. About fame. About fear and happiness. About pain and fairness. It was extraordinary. She taught him to speak and reach out to Cindy. He could talk and provide Cindy comfort. Once again, he was reunited with his beloved wife.

Cindy did not improve with treatment. The chemo stole much of her weight. Her digestive system deteriorated to the extent she couldn't tolerate solid food. They went through a period of admitting and readmitting her to the hospital, until an IV tube became part of her normal apparel. When the pain was bad, she would close her eyes. She only complained about one thing—losing her beautiful hair. It was the most devastating evidence of the chemo's attempt at killing the iniquitous disease. Of all her features, she cherished her hair the most. Stares were no longer at her beauty but at the carnival freak. Eventually she resorted to wearing scarves under the Maple Leaf's cap John had given her.

On more than one occasion, he was surprised when catching his own reflection in a mirror. His once tall, athletic frame had become gaunt. His back hunched. Her disease was physically evident in him, but it changed nothing.

In the last few weeks, she had been confined to a hospital bed, too weak to use the toilet alone. She wanted to fall asleep and not wake up. She was so emaciated that at times John had to leave her side to gain control of his emotions. She resembled the pictures he'd seen of starving Jews in the Nazi death camps. It broke his heart to watch the life fade out of her.

Sometimes he would pretend she was healthy and that it was all a bad dream. For a few magnificent moments, he would recapture his Cindy. Her soft lips, her sweet voice, her joie de vivre. Then with tears close, the façade would crumble, and the almighty present would return. He would squeeze her skeletal fingers lightly; afraid he might crush her bones. She would press back with surprising strength. He would smile; reassured his Cindy still was there.

Every day he would visit with her at the hospital. Some days he went in the morning and stayed all day. He watched her shrink as if the hospital bed was swallowing her up. In time, when the nurses allowed it, he would stay overnight, lying beside her or slumping in the wooden chair next to her bed. Always close enough to hold her slender hand and touch her soft skin.

He continued to see Lauren, absorbing a vitality that helped him get through each darker period.

"You're not hungry?" Lauren asked, twirling a strand of linguine on her fork, now sitting across the table from him in her tiny apartment.

John's thoughts were distant. Creamy Alfredo sauce congealed on his pasta, untouched.

"Sorry," he replied, picking up his fork. "Just thinking."

He slid his fork onto the plate. For a brief moment, he wondered who the woman was sitting across from him.

"God I feel helpless," he said.

Lauren set down her fork. She leaned forward onto her forearms. Her eyes locked on his.

"Want to talk?"

He hesitated. He did. But more than anything, he wanted the hurt to go away.

Before he could respond, Lauren whispered, "It's not fair, John. She's your soul mate."

Her stare made him feel vulnerable. Tears filled her eyes again.

"I love …" Her voice cracked without finishing.

But he knew what she was trying to say.

His vision blurred. His head swam with emotions stretched beyond their limit. He admired her. Relied on her. But love, that was too much.

He had room only for Cindy. She was all he had and wanted. She was everything, and he was losing her.

Life didn't follow the sequence of equations that logic liked to claim it did. There were unknowns without an absolute answer in spite of his beliefs and education to the contrary. There were realities that occurred absent of any reason. They just happened. It often didn't matter what rules were followed with the intention of bringing order to disorder; life happened anyway.

Lauren nodded as John heard the sound of his voice. Again, thinking out loud.

"I'll be here," she said, touching his hand.

"I can't," John replied, the words conveying his honesty. "But thank you."

Lauren forced a poignant smile. She raised her head and lifted her fork. A tear trickled down her cheek.

There was little left to say. Relief passed over him. He needed to go to Cindy's side, to hold her hand and kiss her face. The Cindy he would remember was already gone, but he wanted to be with her for the little time they had left.

As if in answer to his wish, he was with her in their bedroom. Her image was clear, pristine. She was standing in front of their full-length mirror. Hands on her slender hips, wearing faded denims and a red plaid shirt. A smile curved her dark lips as her brown eyes caught his reflection. She was beautiful. She raised her hand and waved.

Then, like a wisp of smoke, her image grew faint and vanished— the magician's job complete.

And he knew.

His fingers pressed into his forehead, trying to hold onto her image as long as he could. God he would miss her. The ache in his gut was unbearable.

He stood up.

"Goodnight, Lauren."

He left her apartment.

Outside, the rain had stopped. The sidewalk was wet.

Mile Eleven

Coming out of Riverview, Tom found himself staring at the dashed line down the center of the road. Funny how rules just became the norm, and drivers conformed. You learned early when starting to drive, not to cross the line. Education, practice, and habit had created a driving culture that developing countries tried to emulate. It was a rule, and everyone who drove knew it. If you broke the rules, there were consequences—and sometimes pain.

There were a lot of rules. He faced them every day. There were the written ones and the unwritten. The company needed them and seemed to revel in their power. To Tom, rules were the culprit of why so few really new ideas made it into production. Most people feared the rules as he did. The unwritten ones being feared the most. "Don't disagree with the boss in a meeting but be open" was like saying, "go swimming but don't go near the water". There was no rule that stated rules had to make sense despite their prolific spread.

The purpose of rules was to avoid mistakes, mistakes that threatened being right and success. Tom knew that. Yet they bred such an aversion to risk and doing things that the biggest achievement for many was just getting through a workday. The risk of taking the wrong step—making the wrong decision—was so distressing that few would make any on their own. He smiled thinking of something he'd heard. *If I don't do anything, I won't make any mistakes. If I don't make any mistakes, I'll be perfect. Therefore, by doing nothing I'll be perfect* … and succeed. It was a ridiculous play on words but he didn't like how it made him feel when he really thought about it. They were all striving for perfection. Follow the rules and you won't make any mistakes. That was the belief, except it was more of a con than a truth. Mistakes *were* made. They happened every day. The irony was that when he did make a mistake, nothing usually happened. He didn't lose his job or even get reprimanded, but he almost always learned something.

With driverlessness, he was learning something every day.

Many had learned how to look and be incredibly busy, convincing themselves of how meaningful their work was. It was the scourge of the corporation. Worst of all, he saw it in himself and hated it.

Tom smiled, thinking of an interview he'd read about a famous movie director whose name escaped him. "What you get fired for when you're young, you win lifetime achievement awards for when you're old."

The prototype for his driverless car was something he'd been working on for a long time. Some days it even replaced his morning workout because he couldn't find time anywhere else. As a kid, he'd built plastic models. Cars mostly, with a few planes and ships thrown in, but cars were his love—both racing and classic. Since then, models had evolved from plastic to die-cast to remote control. Tom became intrigued by the idea that by installing some basic controls and servos, he could make a scaled-down version of a Ferrari or a Porsche—cars he'd dreamed of owning—come to life on the floor. From there it didn't take much to connect the advanced controls the company designed to operate industrial machinery to controlling real cars. With sensor input to an onboard computer, along with data from the Internet and a GPS, cars could drive themselves.

Confronted with the frustration of getting the board interested in anything new, Tom had put together both a working car model and a business plan for how they could approach car manufacturers with a control-based platform for a driverless car.

His model car worked. With the controls and interface in place, he could let it go on the basement floor and watch it drive around by itself. Tom had marveled at the car moving around the basement without hitting anything. Figuring out how to instruct the model on where to go and when seemed almost trivial by comparison.

Tom tightened his grip on the thick rim of the black, leather-wrapped steering wheel and braked for a stop sign. On his right was the four-story apartment building he passed every day on entering the north end of Egan. He looked but saw no one on the balconies that overlooked the highway, anticipating an early riser as the sun came up. Tom accelerated his way through the intersection. In the corner of his eye, he caught the drapes drawn in a second-floor window. He couldn't imagine living in an apartment again.

———◆———

The early-morning sun was beautiful coming through the large picture window. While many blocked the blinding brightness, James was often up early to open the drapes in hopes of catching the sun just above the horizon. Life had changed—a lot. He still was getting used to living in an apartment, for no reason other than his own laziness. Money was not the problem—he now had more than enough—he simply hadn't a reason or the energy to start looking for something new. He pulled the curtain rod sideways as the bright sunshine startled his eyes and warmed his face. The movement of a black BMW on the road caught his eye. Maybe that would be his next car. He'd always wanted to drive the "best engineered car in the world," although he could almost hear his uncle's words refuting it. The thought lasted but an instant as his hand dropped to his side. He turned and looked back at the couch.

James smiled, thinking of the driver of the BMW who was no doubt part of the daily commute in the work world. He thanked God it was no longer his. James's world had changed. There was no less thinking; he just thought about different things.

Like what he was going to do with the secret that he alone knew existed.

Feature No. 3—*Can You Keep a Secret?*

Before I start, you must promise to keep what you're about to read to yourself, or in other words—a secret. Good. I'm glad we have that clear and out of the way. The story involves a hidden national treasure no one knows about—well someone does, otherwise I couldn't tell the story. My intention is to keep it that way. The mere fact of its existence is something quite extraordinary. Unexplainable in many ways, like seeing a ghost, it is as real as my hands and etched into my memory like an image into a piece of glass.

I was nine—old enough to listen to adult conversation but find most of it boring nonsense about politics and bygone eras. Uncle Lou didn't converse much with the adults and was something of a "strange bird," as my father was fond of saying when referring to his brother-in-law. So it surprised me one afternoon when my mother's brother joined my aunt and me for a late lunch. I was in their care while my parents attended an old friend's funeral in England. That day I learned that Uncle Lou had piloted aircraft in the Second World War. During the next hour, he proceeded to captivate me with stories of the war, Europe, and aircraft. It seemed to excite him as much as it did me. He didn't seem as crazy as my father had made him out to be. In fact, he didn't seem crazy at all but more like a genius.

After the war, Uncle Lou had returned to Canada, married my aunt, and returned to school to become a mechanical engineer. He wanted to design and build airplanes and began to talk about "the most amazing aircraft ever built."

At that age, I remembered my confusion as I associated engineers with driving trains, not planes.

"It was unbelievable, Jamie." His eyes lit up like a kid describing a new Lego kit, barely able to sit still. "It was built as a long-range interceptor, capable of speeds up to Mach 2—that's twice the speed of sound."

I stared in wonder across the wood-plank kitchen table, starstruck by this animated person I knew only as weird Uncle Lou. For as long as I could remember, I'd been obsessed with planes and flying. Model airplanes hung on threads from my bedroom ceiling. Books and magazines on aircraft filled my bookshelves.

"Can you imagine traveling as fast as sound?"

In my nine-year-old head, I was trying to imagine how fast that was. I never thought of sound and speed together. It seemed impossible as I heard what he said the same time his lips moved. How did speed come into the picture?

"I remember the day we rolled it out on the tarmac for everyone to see. Lots of important people were there. The company president. The minister of defense. Lots of suits and panache."

He smiled and took a sip from the steaming mug of coffee my aunt had placed in front of him.

"Even your Aunt Bess came to the presentation."

"I knew something was up," Aunt Bess piped in, "because your Uncle Lou bought me a new dress—a fancy red one. But he wouldn't tell me what it was for."

"This wasn't just another plane, Jamie," Uncle Lou said, his thick eyebrows rising. I had turned to face him after listening to Aunt Bess. "This was *real* special. A masterpiece we worked on day and night."

Aunt Bess had little difficulty filling in the pauses between Uncle Lou's sips of coffee.

"There were days," she said, gripping her mug tightly between her hands, "when your Uncle Lou wouldn't get home till after midnight and be gone before I'd even wake up."

"It was the best job I ever had. Couldn't get enough of it. I was young, busting with energy, just like you, working on something we knew was important. We were making history."

Uncle Lou kept smiling.

"It was a fine piece of work—art really—a gorgeous white bird like an angel with sleek wings. The most beautiful thing I'd ever seen—outside of your aunt." His eyes teased across at Aunt Bess sitting next to me. "We designed and built everything right here in Canada. Nothing like it is now. We were going to be the best in the world. We were the best."

"It was your uncle's baby all right," Aunt Bess jumped in as Uncle Lou paused to take a sip of his coffee.

"Jamie," Uncle Lou said, setting down his mug. His demeanor changed as the lines on his forehead flattened. His voice lowered, his tone deepened. I remember being scared, thinking I'd done something to make him mad. It became clear he wanted my full attention. "Can you keep a secret?"

"Yes," I replied, adding further to my excitement that I was about to hear something real special.

His eyes never left mine.

Aunt Bess nodded her head.

"Now, Lou, what kind of a question is that? Of course Jamie can keep a secret." She winked at me.

I nodded.

"Have you ever seen an aircraft up close before? Ever touched one?"

I shook my head. The closest I'd ever been to an airplane was to watch them fly overhead.

"Would you like to?"

"You bet I would!" I shouted.

I'd bugged my mom and dad many times to take me to Malton—Toronto's airport at the time—to watch the airplanes take off and land. I couldn't think of a place I'd rather go. Uncle Lou was just the person to take me too. He might have had his eccentricities, but for a nine-year-old, that spelled fun and adventure not oddness.

"You're sure you can keep a secret?"

"Oh, Lou," Aunt Bess said as I again nodded.

"Come on then," he said, lifting his huge, six-foot-two frame out of the kitchen chair.

I scrambled from my seat behind the table and followed him to the side door.

"Man, this is fantastic!" I cried, running toward his Ford pickup. I seemed to grow a foot taller just thinking about the trip. "A real airplane. That's so cool!"

I pulled open the passenger door and climbed up onto the smooth, black, vinyl bench seat, all ready for the long drive to Malton two hours away. My excitement would make the trip seem endless.

Uncle Lou started the engine, and off we went, but instead of turning out to the road, he swung left and headed off to the back of their property. I kept quiet but couldn't stop my heart from sinking. This was going to be another one of those "misunderstandings" where my youthful exuberance had caused me to misinterpret what was really happening. It had sounded too cool to believe, and what my young mind was already beginning to realize was if it sounded too cool—it likely was. What I had imagined—going up to a real plane and touching it—now seemed pretty farfetched. Closer to the truth was going to be something like Uncle Lou having nailed some boards together in the shape of something resembling an airplane that kids half my age might play with after getting bored with the crate the new refrigerator came in. Dad's description of Uncle Lou's weirdness bubbled to the surface.

As his pickup trundled down the back lane between the poplars, sumac, and maples, I saw the familiar tool shed and garage where Uncle Lou kept his two-tone '57 Chevy and steel-blue, split-window '63 Corvette. With all his oddness, Uncle Lou did manage to have some pretty neat stuff. I couldn't help but wonder how this fit in with airplanes but moved my hand to the door latch as we approached. Maybe he'd painted a big airplane on the side of the tool shed.

With my hand at the ready on the door handle, I waited for the Ford to come to a stop. But the truck kept moving. Its slow, rambling speed over the uneven terrain jostled me back and forth on the seat with no seatbelts. My hand tightened on the metal door handle as we bumped past the front of the garage and kept going. I was surprised we didn't stop. Instead, we passed the side of building where the grass was brown and uncut, in contrast to the well-kept lawn around the house. Ahead of us, I saw two faint paths the width of the truck apart. Uncle Lou didn't hesitate and kept us moving right into them. I could hear long grass scrape the underbelly of the truck and feel the vibration through the floor under my feet. The grass was so long it rose above the front fenders. In all the times I'd been to visit, I'd never been in this area before.

We kept going, through a stand of white birch and small groupings of spruce. My disappointment dissipated as I began to think we might be taking a shortcut to a county road—and a quicker route to the airport.

"Are you sure you can keep a secret?" Uncle Lou asked me again. I thought this must be a route he didn't want anyone else to know about and the reason for the secrecy. Why else would he keep repeating the same question?

"Yes. Mom says I'm real good at secrets."

"Good show."

The Ford carried us into a dim forest, thick with the trunks of pine trees. The coniferous roof blocked out much of the light, yet in amongst nature's fortress emerged a barnlike structure of gray aluminum siding. My eyes grew wide as we moved closer. The air carried the thicker smell of the root-laden and damp forest floor. Trepidation crept into my excitement in this newfound unknown place. I would never have admitted I was scared. But I was now on full alert wondering why this was such a big secret? It was the anxious feeling I got when camping in the backyard where my imagination amplified every sound into something large and monstrous and bad.

Uncle Lou hadn't said a word for several minutes. He was first to break the silence.

"It's been a long time since I brought someone out here, you know," he said, bringing the pickup to a stop alongside the big, silver building. "Nobody knows about this but your aunt and a few special people. Let's go!"

He jumped from the cab like a kid. I could have sworn he looked younger. Gone were the wrinkles in his old leather face. Without closing the truck door, he all but ran to the building. I didn't see a door but watched as he walked up to the outside wall and placed his hand at a certain spot that, as if by magic, opened a small panel and exposed a handle.

"Come on, Jamie! Ain't got all day, you know."

I climbed down from the truck, my reluctance growing. I walked up behind him as he pulled open the hidden door. He directed me to go in. I hesitated but stepped forward. Inside was total darkness. Not a place I would normally go alone. A mixture of gasoline, oil, and grease—the smell of a gas station—replaced the damp, earthy fragrance of the forest. I pictured the garage behind the pumps where my dad filled up his Chevy Caprice.

"Jamie, give me just a second."

My uncle left my side. I stepped from trepidation up to fear. Was he going to leave me alone in this dark place to fend for myself? I don't know why, but I started to count like you do between the flash of lightning and the crash of thunder to measure the proximity of the lightning strike. *One thousand and one, one thousand and two … * but before I got any further, the space before me exploded into light so bright my hands flew up to shield my eyes. But not before I saw the magnificent white aircraft that was lit up in front of me.

It was enormous. The wing tip closest to me might have been ten feet away, but it seemed as if I could have reached out and touched it. The fuselage under the overhead lights was brilliant white. It was the biggest thing my young eyes had ever been that close to. It was huge. It was the first plane I'd ever stood beside in my life. It was amazing!

My uncle said things in the background that I barely heard or for that matter understood.

"The first jet test flew at Mach 1.98, almost two times the speed of sound … only five planes were ever built … this was number six … most believe it was never finished … this is the only one fitted with the Iroquois PS-13 engine … it never officially flew, but if it had, its speed would have reached Mach 3 …"

I stared at its giant call number RL201 on the side of the super-white fuselage. A red maple leaf with a blue circle around it separated the letters from the numbers.

Uncle Lou rhymed off more indecipherable facts.

"Our prime minister stopped the production of these magnificent birds thirteen years ago ... February 20, 1959 ... fourteen thousand people lost their jobs ..."

I moved on legs that were not my own. I stared at the cockpit and walked under the black nose cone with the long, protruding "stinger".

"Diefenbaker was a strange one ... knocked the hell of the country abandoning these planes ... then tried to bring it back together again with the Trans-Canada Highway in '62 ... politicians are a different breed, and they call me crazy ..."

It was like a dream. The plane was more enormous than I could possibly have imagined. As a kid, you don't think about how something can happen. Questions like "How did you get it here?" and "Is it real?" never even occurred to me.

"This *is* the only one in the world ... they destroyed the rest ... it was unbelievable ... like chopping your house up into small pieces ..."

"Can I sit in it?" I asked. In seconds, a metal stairway appeared in front of me. I climbed up into the cockpit. The smell of oiled leather and old metal was magical. There were more dials and switches than I could count, and I wanted to touch every one of them. At nine years old, it wasn't the technology or the design that impressed me, but simply that I was in the most amazing toy in the world.

I don't remember how I got home from that trip or much of what happened afterward. I do remember Uncle's Lou's bearded face looking down at me from the top of the cockpit, saying, "You mustn't speak of this to anyone."

One day not long after my visit, I was looking through some aviation books at our public library. I saw Uncle Lou's plane. And then I knew.

I smiled, knowing my uncle would be proud that his secret was safe with me forever.

Uncle Lou and Aunt Bess left their entire estate to me.

This is the first time I've ever told this story. Remember, it's a secret, so don't tell a soul. You promised.

Mile Fifteen

As the sky grew brighter, a few more cars appeared on the empty roads. The world was waking up. The BMW followed the right curve out of Egan and was soon back into rural country again. A galvanized-steel guardrail, which kept out-of-control motorists from going over the dangerous drop beside the road, passed on his right. The rail was shiny-new. Tom couldn't remember noticing it before. So much of what he drove by every day went by like that.

Passing the safety rail triggered Silke back into his thoughts—whose mere glance could distract him from whatever he was doing. He was supposed to meet her for coffee after work—to discuss the team—prompting him to take another drink of his coffee. His intentions were a bit more than that if he was truthful with himself. The fantasy of being with such a beautiful woman was hard to resist. Her toned, golden arms and wisps of blonde hair that curled up her smooth cheeks so tempting to touch. He wasn't inviting her for purely altruistic reasons, but the issues with the team were real. She could help if he could curb his distraction. Would he go further if the opportunity arose? His curiosity beckoned, but he decided not to go there. She was part of his team.

And why didn't the team work better together?

"The whole must be greater than the sum of the parts" repeated in his head as it often did when he asked himself this question. A functioning team was more than a group of people just sitting together. It was engaged people that made things happen, not processes and rules. Leaders knew this. It was part of who they were. No one did anything alone—except enter and exit this world. Any kind of success was built on bringing people together in a common cause. Those who figured that out were the real leaders. He could do that. In fact had done it before. But now the company wanted him to work in a different way—a puppet he couldn't be.

For many team members, their work had become a game of comparison or "who knew the most" that created all kinds of disruption. Competing on who was smarter or knew more drove Tom crazy. Self-defeating and petty, it missed the point of what they were there to do—to create something of value. Their competition was beyond the company's walls—not inside—and needed everything they could give it and more. Yet the energy of competing to be the "smartest" sucked much of that away. The game was exacerbated by the ambiguity and confusion of what they were working on, which only served to heighten Tom's drive to push driverlessness even more.

Further compounding the team's misfortune was the not-so-subtle change in responsibility from product development into ensuring the new product delivered on its financial goals. It wasn't explained that way, but that's what it amounted to. Tom hated it. It wasn't what he was about. It was short-term thinking and unsustainable. In the past, he'd left it alone, confident it would figure itself out. But it wasn't happening this time. Faith that it would was fading. Did he really have the stamina to keep trying and—more importantly—the inclination?

Expectations of the group and what they reported on had changed too. What was once the means to an end was becoming the end in itself. Now instead of creating new products, executives and managers were asking for schedules and metrics and mission statements that required endless charts and graphs and reports to quantify progress. Managing updates had become more important than the value of whatever they were creating. The new product was nothing more than a few modifications on something old—not something really new. Would they fool anyone? To add further insult, no one seemed to understand what he was talking about with driverlessness and what it could mean to their future. "It isn't our business," he heard time and time again. Now he found himself in the uncomfortable position of trying to sell, promote, and lead a program his heart wasn't in.

It was little wonder the team was struggling. Outside of cost reduction, there wasn't much to add. They were creating a new product without any latitude to define or create the product.

"This isn't development—it's fucking babysitting," a frustrated team member had said. Tom found it hard to disagree.

How had he turned things around before? There was always a heartbeat in there somewhere. The difference this time was the heart he kept coming back to wasn't beating, and the heart that was wasn't aligned with what the board wanted. It was like trying to escape from an Escher drawing. It filled most of his waking mind and was eating into his sleeping one. This morning's early wakeup was happening all too often.

He took a sip of coffee and saw Silke's lean, muscular legs. Sweet.

So much of what he believed in—running a business, creating a new product—did not align with his thoughts of Silke. At one moment, he was extoling the purity and virtue of creativity and innovation to create a better future and the next considering actions that were contrary to being a good human being.

Humans were the only creatures in the animal kingdom given keys to unlock the vast nature of the mind's imagination yet so often overruled by the raw animal instinct that otherwise drove their actions.

Why was this happening?

Because he'd led himself here. He'd let himself be led. He was bored. His mind wasn't expanding. He needed to create and invent. He believed that to create something of true value required touching humans in a profound way. But that wasn't what his work had become. Life was passing by. He was following the rules—following orders. But he wasn't built that way. Was anyone? He had succumbed to rules and orders because that was how it worked or was supposed to. Because it was the right thing to do or what he'd been told was the right thing. Given enough time and force, humans could adjust to anything—and he could too. For him, building a life had stopped when it got too tough. It had led him to considering actions that would mess up all he really cared about.

He slowed the BMW as he approached a school zone on the main street of Oak Bridge—*Blink and you can miss this town*, he thought. On his left were a number of two-story buildings: a convenience store, a coffee shop, and a used bookstore. The second floors likely housed apartments. Above the convenience store was a lone window that was always lit in the morning when he passed. He couldn't remember it ever being dark. Yet like much of what he passed every day, he knew nothing of what went on inside.

Strange that something so familiar could be so unknown at the same time—the paradox wasn't missed on him.

The small town left his thoughts before he exited its southern boundary. He never talked of it. Outside of driving through the town every day, it rarely entered his mind. It was something akin to going to the movies and trying to remember the trailers before the feature. He never remembered them all without prompting. Then as if triggered by the same thought, he caught the dark rectangle of the long abandoned Aryn Drive-In theatre—a relic from years past—in the distance. The once cool way to see the movies with your sweetheart was now all but a dilapidated giant wall of plywood boards.

A few minutes farther south, he missed the light at Highway 8 and had to bring the BMW to a full stop. There was a touch of irony having to do so when no other cars were around. But he just couldn't bring himself to go through the red light. He smiled as a Ford Mustang coming from the west had to come to a stop as the light changed again. There was no justice.

As he brought the BMW back up to speed, a little over the posted limit, he had to slow again as a raccoon crossed the road ahead of him. He didn't often see wildlife anymore. The road was too busy. But every now and then, an animal would emerge. They would appear and vanish so quickly as really not to be seen at all. Yet still they marked his memory. Sometimes he would remember during lunch or a break, prompted by someone else's story. He hardly had his foot back on the accelerator when he slowed again as the speed limit dropped for the small town of Aryn. A young man was climbing into a late-model GMC pickup that was idling in a short driveway near the road. The man was carrying a black leather satchel.

———◆———

Tony had seen the black BMW round the corner. It wasn't the first time he'd seen it pass. He didn't know whether it was the same one he'd see pass in the evening going the other way but thought it was quite likely. Like how many black BMWs drove through Aryn? He'd loved cars for as long as he could remember. BMWs always caught his eye. He didn't know whether it was from the ads for German engineering or the styling, but there was something that attracted him to the car. Maybe it was the prestige they represented—the sense of having made it. He didn't know. But maybe where they were headed today would bring him another step closer to owning one.

A lot had happened.

Feature No. 4—*Devon Tower*

"Hold on!" Tony screamed into the microphone. He held the note in key with the fuzz of Denver's sustained G coming through the Marshall cabinet. Their final note faded into the cheering late-night crowd.

"Thank you! Thank you very much!" Tony shouted into his mike over the loud ovation.

The Building was packed despite it being half an hour past last call. It was a good night. Lots of chicks. Lots of noise. Lots of excitement. And two record company reps. Rock and roll was alive and kickin' ass. They had given the crowd, the two from the record company, and anyone else who cared to listen a taste of what Atlantis was all about. Tonight they were on fire. They were tight and connected. The crowd's response was confirmation of that. It made up for all the bullshit in setting up and tearing down. It made the endless hours of travel, practice, and preparation worth the sacrifice. It was what they lived for. It brought meaning to their lives.

"Fuckin' awesome!" screamed Denver as he jumped off the stage behind the stacked Marshalls. "Unbelievable!"

Dave threw his drumsticks to a couple of gushing teenage girls at the side of the stage and then disappeared. He never made it back to the office they were using as a makeshift dressing room.

"Fuckin' eh!" agreed Tony, unslinging his Rickenbacker bass and setting it on the stand at the corner of the stage. "Good-bye, day jobs."

Bbbbzzzzzz!

Tony's eyelids flashed open. His alarm. On reflex, his hand batted his electric wakeup off. The room returned to silence.

Sally was asleep beside him. His mind was foggy, yet his thoughts came quickly. Sally had come out to see them play for the first time in months. They had been late getting home from The Building. Even later getting to sleep. They had both had a lot to drink. He still could feel that. But what the hell, they had a lot to celebrate.

He had to pick up Denver. They were downtown today. They'd started a new contract.

How could it be quarter to six already? He had just put his head on the pillow; his ears still were ringing from their last set.

The air was chilly. Just a few more minutes, he thought. Who would know the difference? It was tempting.

———◆———

Cough. Cough.

"Daddy, *Sadurday*?"

Emmy was at his bedside. Her croup sounded in his ear. It seemed as though she'd been sick for weeks. One thing after another. Ear infection. Running nose. Sore throat. Now coughing, coughing, coughing.

Tony's thoughts drifted.

Things were coming together. A deal was on the horizon, promising money and steady work on the road. "They want to sign Atlantis," Alan, their manager, had said while they sipped double espressos at two in the morning. He had winked and nodded at Sally. "These boys are ready to explode."

Sally knew it too and smiled.

Tony sat up. What time was it! The clock read 6:30 a.m. It wasn't the weekend! His mind was racing. Last night ... Thursday night ... they played ... today was ...

"Daddy ..."

"No!" he cried.

He was late. His intention of closing his aching eyes for a few more minutes had failed. It seemed impossible for forty-five minutes to have passed.

He threw off the comforter. He was supposed to pick Denver up at six thirty. Denver would be pissed.

"Tony, aren't you—"

"Late for fucking work!" he snapped back. Sally sat up. Emmy started to cry. His frantic movement frightened her.

"It's okay, sweetie. Daddy's late," whispered Sally. Emmy climbed into her mother's arms.

Tony pulled on the jeans from the floor that he'd worn the day before. He searched for a shirt in the dirty clothes hamper beside their battered bureau. Grabbing a red T-shirt, he gave his girls kisses good-bye and ran out of the room.

He felt like shit. His head pounded from the exploits of only a few hours earlier. His eyes burned like his pupils were hot embers. It would be another endless day.

He padded down the stairs, grabbed his Budweiser cap from the kitchen counter, and headed out the door.

Outside, the world was lightening; dawn was hinting on the horizon. Tony scrambled to put the key in the ignition switch of his ten-year-old Ford pickup. He was going to hear shit today and not just from Denver. Hank, their crew boss, was his biggest worry. A week ago, Hank had set down the law: if anybody was late at the new site, they might as well turn around and go home. He wasn't going to tolerate any more lateness. Tony and Denver had been the culprits—coming straight from an out-of-town gig. This new job was tight and had to finish on time—and they would be on time if Hank had to hire a whole new crew. He was already on their case about their double life. If they wanted work, ditch the guitars; otherwise he'd replace them.

Tony stomped on the accelerator. The rear tires squealed to life. There was no way they would make it by seven.

"Where the fuck have you been!" snarled Denver, shoving his aluminum lunchbox onto the floor of the cab. He climbed in and sat on the worn bench seat. Tony doubted Denver had been to bed.

"Sorry, bud," Tony said, gunning the pickup back onto the road. Thirty minutes would get them downtown. It was quarter to seven.

"I didn't think you were serious last night," Denver replied, fastening his seatbelt.

"He won't fire us."

"He'll be firin' our asses good. He's been waiting for this day to come."

With that, Denver pulled the brim of his Boston Bruins baseball cap over his bloodshot eyes.

"Wake me up when we're there."

Tony was certain he saw a glint of satisfaction cross Denver's unshaven face. Denver enjoyed watching him sweat, especially when it was out of his hands. Denver hadn't wanted the job in the first place. He hated getting up before noon. He'd agreed to work contract to pay his share of the equipment rentals—but it was a temporary thing, not a career. He was carefree and without responsibilities. "Why complicate it?" was his motto. He lived in a sparsely furnished bachelor apartment and survived on a meager inheritance his grandmother had left him. If he needed something above the cost of food or rent, he went without. Tony was amazed when Sally found out that Denver didn't eat for two days to save enough to buy a new effects pedal.

Speed limit signs flew by, marking speeds well below what they were traveling at. By seven ten, they were more than halfway. With luck, they'd be there in twenty minutes.

As they came into the heart of the city, the buildings grew taller and became the sky-scraping towers of downtown. Looking up from street level, the buildings were so close together as to almost resemble tunnels to the sky.

Denver's breathing passed from mild rumblings to heavy snoring. Tony envied him. It was all he could do to keep his own eyes open— thankful the pounding behind them had relented. Sleep was priceless when he'd only banked a couple of hours.

Denver lifted his cap as they pulled off University onto King. Tony drove into Devon Tower's underground parking designated for maintenance vehicles. There was a lump in his throat as he pulled in beside an old, rusty Cavalier. He looked around, but Hank's green Econoline was nowhere in sight. The clock on the dashboard read 7:32.

Denver turned. His voice was groggy. "He's not here."

He opened the passenger door and climbed out.

"Greg's here," he said, slamming the door shut. Greg's familiar white Camaro was parked in the corner. Denver pulled his safety harness out of the back of the pickup. On big jobs like Devon Tower, the building's maintenance department supplied the big equipment and subcontracted the labor. Usually a crew only had to show up with their safety harnesses and go to work.

They made their way to the service elevator that took them to the main lobby, where they checked in with security. They took another elevator to the roof. On exiting, they found Greg standing in the service hallway with his back against the wall. A cigarette drooped from his lips.

"Where the hell you going!" Hank bellowed from behind them. Tony's heart stopped as his bowels loosened.

They both turned like trained dogs. Hank looked as if he had just climbed out of bed. Tufts of uncombed gray hair stuck out like wings behind his ears. Several days' growth of black stubble covered his jaw. Denver stepped back into the elevator as the doors began to close. He raised his hand in a departing gesture, wincing. Tony stuck his arm between the closing doors.

"To wash some windows," Tony replied, his eyes fixed on Hank's as the elevator doors retracted. Denver shot him the finger.

"Why the fuck are you late?"

"Missed my alarm," Tony answered before he had time to think of anything else.

His brain went into double time. They were half the crew. Hank never stepped on the swing platform. If he wanted to clean windows today, he needed both of them. If they were fired, they wouldn't be talking.

"The fuck you did!"

Hank glared at Tony. One bushy eyebrow rose. The gesture was like watching someone cock the trigger of a gun.

"We're here now."

Hank nodded at the elevator.

"What's your buddy got to say?"

"I's waitin' for Tony," Denver answered, his voice much quieter than his screams backstage. He glowered at Tony.

"Maybe it's time you bought a fuckin' car?"

Denver said nothing.

Hank moved closer. He had a way of making people feel diminutive despite his five-foot-six height. What he lacked in physical size his booming voice made up for, exploding the air around them.

"What! Are you waitin' for me to fire your asses!" he bellowed as he passed between them. "Well!"

Tony made for the door opposite Greg, relieved. Enough said. Their jobs were safe for another day. He wasn't about to try the man's patience further. Denver was right behind him.

"Next time, girls," Hank yelled after them, "stay at the coffee shop."

Neither of them slowed until they were up on the roof with the sun beaming in their faces. Nothing blocked the sun forty-six stories up. They joined Liz and Jordan, who were rigging the platform near the side of the roof. Tony peered over the edge. A panoramic view of Toronto harbor spread out in front of him. Despite his tiredness, he could not ignore the magnificence—another day with the gods. There was nothing that beat the view up high. There were days, standing near the edge of a roof, he would stretch out his arms like Jack Dawson on the front of the *Titanic* and believe he could fly.

Words came to him as he looked out over Lake Ontario. He reached in his back pocket for his coil-ringed notepad, whispering the words.

I don't need a compass for believing
I'm headed where my eyes are seeing.

But his pad wasn't there. In his haste to leave, he had left it on his nightstand.

In a mild panic, he turned to Denver.

"Got any paper?"

Denver shrugged and stuffed his hands in the front pockets of his jeans. He held up a receipt and passed it to Tony.

"A pen?"

Denver shook his head. "You're the writer."

"Liz'll have one."

Tony walked to where Liz was standing beside Jordan, coiling a rope on the swing platform they would soon descend down the side of Devon Tower in. Liz was Hank's daughter. Not yet twenty, she made the confrontations with Hank almost worth the effort. She easily could step off the pages of *Esquire* or *Maxim*. Five foot two and maybe 105 pounds after a big meal, she bore no resemblance to her father. They'd all concluded she wasn't biologically his kid. He was mean, fouled-mouthed, and ugly; she was even-tempered, pleasant, and gorgeous. She was blonde with a light tan; he was dark and gray-haired. She was tying off one of the safeties as Tony approached.

"Hi, Liz," he greeted her back. She was good to look at from any direction. Her faded cutoffs showed off the full length of her toned legs that would be heaven to touch.

"Mornin', Anthony," she replied without turning around. She was the only one that called him that. He liked it.

He could feel the words he wanted to write down fading. They usually didn't stick around for long.

"Can I borrow your pen for a minute?"

"Sure," she answered, pulling the ballpoint clipped to the collar of her T-shirt that read *Window Wash Her?* "What's up?"

"Ah, just somethin' I don't want to forget." He took the pen.

She smiled. Her teeth were white and perfect. He looked away, knowing her blue eyes would steal away any hope he had of getting the words in his head down on paper. He searched for a hard surface to write on.

"My clipboard's on the side of the jib," she told him.

"Thanks," he said, surprised. "I hope you can't read anything else I'm thinking."

Smiling again, she said nothing and turned back to her duties.

He wrote down the words as he remembered them. Two more lines followed.

Follow most at the split ahead,
I turned the other way instead.

He hardly had the words down when the tune started. If only he had his six-string. Melodies stayed with him if he could see them on the fingerboard—a visual-sound thing. Beside the words he jotted down a few letters, each signifying the chord sequence. The tune in his head matched the letters. He wrote down the last letter as Hank came up behind him.

"Writin' your last will and testament?" he asked, chuckling. "You might need it today."

Tony huffed out a laugh and tucked the song in the front pocket of his jeans. The words were the semblance of a new song destined to be a hit. He felt that way about every song he wrote.

"Well, girls," Hank announced, hands on his waist, "let's get the show on the road."

This was the first cleaning contract Hank had won for a building as large as Devon Tower. He had told them this was the first of several "big" contracts he was negotiating. There was a lot of work downtown if they didn't screw it up.

The swing platform—or "gone-dola" as Denver preferred to call it—was all aluminum construction. Though well-used and dirty from the paint and grime that spotted the rails and floor, the structure looked solid. Two rails—an upper and lower—ran the periphery of the platform. Wire mesh covered the space in between to the floor—to prevent their tools from becoming deadly projectiles to pedestrians passing below. The jib cranes that lowered the platform into position down the side of the tower were robust fixtures. Provisions in the roof anchored the cranes on all four sides of the building. The arrangement was a marked improvement over some of the sites they'd worked on. They were well secured.

Liz was the first to move, climbing into her customary center position on the platform. Already wearing her Skygenie harness, she snapped a carabiner onto the safety line that ran the length of the platform. As she tied off her ropes, Denver swung his leg over the platform's aluminum railing at one end and fastened himself in. Tony did the same at the other end.

Jordan operated the crane control while Greg handed out the two-way radios. Each checked to ensure their radio worked and was secured to the chest strap of their safety harness. It was Greg's responsibility to double check that everyone's harness was secured to the safety lines running the length of the platform and fastened in position. When everyone was ready, Jordan took over.

For Tony, this was the worst part. Jordan would raise the gondola a couple of feet off the rooftop and then maneuver them out over the side. Once they were off the ground, Jordan took a moment to check things. This check was the only time Tony considered the dangers they were exposed to. His brain seemed to overcompensate for the position of his center of gravity and caused him a brief moment of vertigo. Once he started working, he forgot how high they were above the streets below. His mind would drift to thoughts of Sally and Emmy, the band and their future.

As they swung over the edge, they gave the all-clear thumbs up to begin their descent. Today, a mild breeze blew through his hair. It wasn't enough to bother them. They dropped down four rows of windows and carried on from where they'd left off the day before.

"I'm surprised you're still alive," Liz said. She was always the first to speak when they were out on the wall out of earshot of her father. "He was really pissed at you this morning."

She laughed, knowing her father sparked fear in all of them.

"Slept pass my alarm," Tony confessed.

"I'll bet," Denver said. He was shaking his head. "More like some early-morning nookie if you ask me."

"Yeah right," Tony shot back.

"How'd it go last night?" Liz asked. She knew about Atlantis. Had even come out to see them play.

"We had a great night!" Denver said, wiping his squeegee across his thigh. "Record deals, screaming chicks, hot licks ..."

Liz looked at Denver and then over at Tony, with her eyes rolled to the sky.

"Where'd you get this guy?"

"He was standing on a corner. Said he could play the guitar."

"Yeah," Denver shouted back, "but you said you were a musician."

"So, Denver, what's the deal?" Liz said, squeaking her squeegee down the window.

"Deal?" Denver asked, turning to look at her.

"Yeah, why don't you have a car?"

"'Cause they won't give him a license," Tony answered. He pointed toward his friend, holding his wipe rag out like a flag. "Would you give him a fuckin' license?"

"I think of it as a higher state of being," Denver responded, tilting his head upward with an air of feigned self-importance.

"It's a higher level, all right," Tony said. "Right up there in the fuckin' clouds."

Liz laughed.

"I can't believe you two haven't killed each other."

"Killin' 'im would ruin all the fun," Denver quipped. "Besides, how would I get to work?"

"Good question," Tony shot back. Then attempting to have the last word added, "but a better one might be how you're getting home."

"Liz said she'd drop me off," Denver said, not missing a beat.

Liz turned toward Denver with a look of disdain and then glanced back at Tony with one eyebrow raised and a smirk on her face.

"I don't imagine Daddy'll mind."

She giggled, getting to play a part in their banter.

"How's everythin' goin' down there!" Hank yelled. He was thirty feet overhead, looking down over the edge of the roof. He seemed to know he'd been brought into the conversation.

"Great," answered Liz on behalf of the three of them.

"I'm taking off," Hank replied. He was holding a handset but talking directly down at them. "Keep the girls in line."

"Count on it," Liz answered, giving her father the thumbs up.

Hank disappeared. They were on their own. It was the best time of the day.

They finished their first row of windows. Denver requested they be lowered. Denver's "gone-dola" descended as the winch above unwound the cables. The windows appeared to rise beside them.

They repeated the routine of cleaning a row of windows and dropping to the next two more times in relative quiet. Tony kept adding lines to his song, becoming increasingly frustrated not having his notepad and having to squeeze the words onto the small paper receipt. But the words kept coming.

No one's with me, I'm on my own
The untraveled road of virgin stone

He mouthed the words, grappling for a way to remember them.

Don't know what stands in my way
It's the only route for me to stay

He did not want to go further. Any more and he would surely forget something. He repeated the words again and again, searching for the tune. There had to be a hook, something to bring it together. It was coming. He could feel it.

"Shit!" cursed Denver, jerking Tony from his thoughts. "Fuck!"

"Fuck, Denver, what's your problem?"

The words he was memorizing vanished like a wisps of smoke into the breeze.

"Fucking knife!"

"Oh my god!" Liz shouted.

The platform shook. Tony turned and saw Liz, already unhooked, rushing toward Denver's end of the platform. Denver was holding his arm out. Blood covered his hand.

Tony keyed his radio. "Greg, I think we need to come up. Denver's cut. Stand by."

"Ten-four. Is he okay?"

"Dunno."

Tony's hand went to his safety—and hesitated. *Never unhook when you're out there,* whispered a voice in the back of his head. It would be okay; Denver was in trouble.

"Got a fucking clean rag?" Liz said as he moved in behind her. "He's really bleeding."

Tony pulled a piece of white cotton fabric, once the sleeve of a dress shirt, out of his side pouch.

"What the fuck were you doin'?" Tony fired off, trying to lighten the moment. He could see the blood streaming from his friend's wrist.

"Fuckin' plastic wrap ... I was opening a new scraper," Denver answered. His voice was shaky.

While he listened, Tony pulled the belt out of his pants. He was no doctor but was pretty sure Denver had sliced an artery. He needed a tourniquet.

"The fucking knife slipped," Denver went on. "I'm such an idiot."

"Can't disagree with that," Tony joked, but there was no laughter in his voice. He squeezed between Liz and the railing. For an instant, he thought of tying off his safety. But the thought left as quickly as it came. He wrapped the belt around Denver's arm and looped it through the buckle, then pulled it tight.

"Hold onto this and don't let go," he instructed his friend, noticing his red T-shirt. "You should be wearing my fucking shirt."

Add pressure flashed through his brain from a first aid course he'd taken eons ago to become a lifeguard.

"Liz, hold the rag as tightly as you can against his wrist."

"I am!" she shouted.

Tony heard the panic in her voice. He put his hand on her shoulder. He couldn't remember ever touching her before.

"Just hold it tight," he whispered as much to reassure her as himself.

He hooked in his harness and looked for Liz's. Standing up, he keyed his radio.

"Get us up, now!" he shouted into the radio.

"Roger, ten-four," Greg replied.

The cables tightened as Jordan activated the controls. The platform stiffened and began to move. The tightness in Tony's stomach eased. He saw Liz was still unhooked.

The platform jarred to a stop. He reached to grab her and at the same time took hold of the railing to stay upright.

"What the hell!" he yelled at his radio.

An uncomfortable silence followed.

"Fuck, Jordan, get us up!" he shouted.

Tony was sure he could hear the whine of the winch's motor overhead, but the platform wasn't moving.

"Fuck, Liz, hook in!" he yelled at her.

For the first time, he felt the platform swing away from the building. The knot in his stomach regained its tightness.

He keyed his radio.

"Jordan!" he said, his voice hard and serious. He spoke slowly. "Get us the fuck up!"

"Sorry," Greg responded. "He's working on it. Something's jammed."

Liz was holding Denver's wrist. Not only was she not hooked in, her harness was off. Tony looked to the center of the platform. Amazingly, her harness was hanging on the safety line. *How did he miss it?* She would have to go back to get hooked in.

"Liz!" he yelled, this time feeling panic circling. "Get your fucking harness on!"

She turned.

"Okay already!" she shouted. "I heard you the first time."

Tony didn't care about hurt feelings at this point. He was thankful Liz was moving.

Denver was pale. Blood now covered his hands, pants, and shirt. Liz had his blood on her T-shirt and shorts along with her work boots. Tony found another clean rag and wrapped it around the crimson one Liz already had in place. He replaced her hold on his friend's injured wrist, keeping pressure on the wound.

"I didn't know you cared," Denver joked, his voice weak but his sense of humor still intact.

Again the platform shifted. Only then did Tony realize how unbalanced they'd made the platform by moving around. Maybe they had simply overloaded the winch.

"Try her again!" he shouted into his radio, "Maybe the ..."

Tony heard it before he felt it—the gut-wrenching groan of the metal structure flexing beneath his feet. The air-ripping twang of the steel cable as it whizzed past them, ready to slice-through anything in its path.

There was no time to do anything but hold on. Both Denver and Tony were hooked in. Liz was not so fortunate. She was inches from her harness, but that was as close as she got. Like Tony and Denver, she fell to the floor as the platform swung downward. Then, too rattled to get a handhold, she slid down the sloping floor of the platform into the two men. Only Tony's quick reaction to grab her bloodied T-shirt kept her from plummeting the forty stories to the ground.

She screamed. Her eyes burned into Tony's. Her arms and legs flailed in every direction.

Though his safety was latched, Tony could feel himself sliding out of the platform too. Only the grip his left hand had on the steel mesh between the rails kept him in the gondola. His right hand was locked onto the front of Liz's T-shirt, all but pulling it off as she dangled over the platform's railing. Her weight was pulling him out. His harness cut painfully into his shoulders. His arm was stretched. How long his shoulder would stay in its socket was only a guess.

Terrified, Liz kept screaming.

"Liz!" Tony shouted. "You have to stop moving!"

Please let me hold on, he prayed, the pain in his shoulder already near unbearable.

He focused on Liz's blonde hair flowing behind her head—anything to distance the pain.

Liz stopped shaking. In disbelief, he watched her hands grab hold of his forearm.

"Ahhhh!" he yelled as her nails sunk into his skin.

There was no movement in his arm, yet he could feel her slipping away. Then he saw why. Her T-shirt was tearing.

"Stop!" he yelled, but Liz could do nothing but hold onto his forearm. He had to think of something else. He didn't dare let go of the railing with his other hand or he'd be over it in a second. The harness might hold him, but he doubted it would hold them both. Any movement might sever their hold on each other.

"I can't get my ..."

Despite the lock-hold he had on her T-shirt, the shirt continued to rip apart. The shoulder seam was stretched further than he would have thought possible. Her hands were sliding down his forearm, her fingernails gouging his flesh. The scene was unimaginable yet magnified in clarity.

Her screams were inhuman. Feeling the material tear was absolute terror.

Tony loosened his hand on the mesh, thinking it might help. But he felt his body shift as he did.

"God, please ... let me ..."

He was on the edge of going over. The fingers of his left hand retightened on the mesh, the wire cutting into his skin like he was holding knife blades. But he stopped his slide over the rail.

Liz's fingernails continued to gouge into his forearm. He became numb to the pain. He was helpless to stop her as she dangled four hundred feet above the street below.

The T-shirt continued to tear.

Her hands reached his clenched fist. She stopped sliding—his fist, like a knot in a rope, giving her a firmer handhold.

Liz was holding on.

Then, with the nonchalance of letting a bird fly out of her hands, her grip released.

For Tony, time stopped as he watched her be pulled out to sea, never to be seen again.

His eyes closed. He did not listen for the impact.

As if his life had been taken, he hung over the side of the disabled gondola numb to the world.

At first he didn't notice the dripping on his left arm. The feel of something trickling down his bicep caused him to open his eyes. The remnant of Liz's bloodied T-shirt was clenched in his hand. Terror shot through his body. Reflex shook his hand. Yet his fist stayed tight, unable to release the material or his muscles. His arm was locked straight.

He let go of the lower railing and saw blood on his left arm. It didn't match the color of his shirt after all.

But how …

Before he had the answer, his weight shifted. He was going over the rail.

The disabled gondola swung like a macabre pendulum back and forth on its remaining cable. On its return swing, Tony was able to transfer enough of this weight to grab hold of the top rail with his left hand. He used his right hand, still full of white T-shirt, as best he could to push himself back. His harness was on, but he had no intention of tempting his fate any further.

The agony in his right arm would have kept him still under most circumstances, until he saw Denver's pallid face above him. His friend was hanging from his safety harness. His slashed arm was at his side, dripping blood onto Tony and now the gondola. The belt—Tony's belt—was gone from his arm.

It was only then Tony noticed the wide, startled eyes staring at them through the building's windows. Someone had a video camera up against the glass. They were live entertainment—reality TV.

"Denver!" Tony shouted.

Denver didn't move or make any indication he'd even heard his friend's shout.

On seeing people close by, a new clearness returned to Tony's head. He edged himself back against the floor of the gondola that was now close to vertical. His work boots rested on the wire mesh as the gondola's motion slowed.

"You mothafucker!" Tony screamed, hoping to startle his friend out his semi-conscious state.

Denver stirred and moved his head sideways.

"Come on, buddy!" Tony yelled. "Don't fail me now!"

He was a couple of feet from Denver's dangling boot. He looked away and again saw Liz's bloodied cotton T-shirt in his hand.

Determined, he ground his teeth as he looked at his injured arm. It was difficult to believe it was his—his hand was so white. Bleeding gouges ran down his forearm to his wrist. He turned away. It hurt to look. With his good hand, he pulled himself upright, his feet on the steel mesh. His safety rope chafed the side of his face. For a moment, he let go of the steel mesh and rubbed his clenched hand to get it working. He discarded the remains of Liz's T-shirt and let it drop to the mesh. It didn't seem real; it couldn't be all part of the same dreadful nightmare. He fought his own conscious state.

Good-bye, Elizabeth passed his lips in silent prayer.

Tony would have to climb part way up the steel mesh of the angled gondola to get in position to help Denver. He raised his injured arm, fighting the gnawing pain in his shoulder. With his left hand, he reached up as high as he could and pulled. He could do it. Feeling came back into his right hand. He tried to pull with it but found he couldn't. He needed another good hand. He let go.

"Fucking help us!" he screamed at the people behind the windows.

He looked toward the roof but saw no one. From below came the sirens. For a crazy moment, he wondered what they were for. Shock was hovering, edging him closer to hysteria.

Control, remember control.

A splash of blood landed on his injured arm. With it came an idea. As before, he hoisted himself up with his good arm. Then with everything he had, he held himself with his bad arm. With his left arm, again he hauled himself up until his face was even with his hand. Denver didn't move, hanging like a corpse from a noose. Denver's safety rope was pressed hard against his face.

"Denver!" he shouted.

Denver blinked his eyes, too weak to move.

"Fuck, buddy, don't give up!" Tony yelled, trying to keep his balance.

He saw the radio attached to Denver's harness and realized his was gone. It explained why he wasn't hearing anything from the roof. He again heard the shriek of sirens below bouncing off the glass buildings. He refused to think about what they were responding to.

He looked to the top of the building. Despite the agony in his arm, he tightened his hold on the steel mesh between the rails. He had to get to a higher position to stop Denver's bleeding. He transferred more weight to his bad arm, stoking the fire in his shoulder.

His eyes caught the flash of something at the window. Someone held up a sign: *the rope is breaking.* Several people—not ten feet away, with their feet planted firmly on solid ground—were pointing at something above him. He looked up at Denver's safety rope. The line was fraying over the edge of the aluminum platform. If that broke, he'd lose Denver too.

Denver's head slumped sideways.

"Fucking help us!" Tony yelled.

As he heard his own words, his grip tightened on the mesh.

Why wasn't someone trying to pull them up?

Denver's arm was his target, but he needed a tourniquet. He looked down at his utility belt still in place. A leather lace ran through a hole in the handle of his squeegee. He pulled the tool from his belt, untied the lace, and let the squeegee fall onto the mesh below. Ignoring the tightening pain in his shoulder, he pulled himself up on the wire meshing. Then holding the mesh with one hand, he slipped the leather strap around Denver's forearm, crossed it, put one end between his teeth, and pulled. Still holding the steel mesh with his hand in agony, he yanked the lace tight, pulling Denver's limp arm with it. He crossed the ends again and pulled the knot tight with his teeth.

With Denver's blood flow stopped, Tony braced himself against his friend to think of what to do about the precarious condition of their safety line.

He wanted to scream. Scream at the forces that seemed so against them. Scream at the time that was running out. Scream because he was so close to losing control. Panic had its suffocating arms all but wrapped around him.

Give me something …

The air shifted, swaying the gondola away from the building like they were pieces hanging from a giant child's mobile. Something stirred beside him like the flutter of a bird in a bush. He turned and stared into the face of a woman whose red-lipped mouth was wide. She was jumping up and down, pointing at something through the window.

Tony turned his head and saw the rope hanging not two feet from his side.

Without thinking, he let go of Denver and grabbed the rope as another fell beside him. His right arm screamed as he clung to the mesh.

Shifting his weight, he grabbed hold of the rope with his left hand. Tucking the rope in beside his right arm, he pulled himself a little higher on the steel mesh, forgetting his torn hand. He looped the rope under Denver's one arm, across his chest, and under his other arm. He struggled to double-knot the rope behind Denver's head with one hand but finally had it. With Denver tied, he wrapped his arm in the other rope.

Then, as if misfortune was timed to his efforts, Denver dropped.

It happened in an instant like the fall of an icicle from the edge of an eave trough on a warm winter's day. Tony didn't have time to close his eyes or look away.

Denver dropped but a foot before the rope from above caught his full weight. There was a God.

Tony closed his eyes, let go of the mesh, and held on. The rope wrapped around his arm held him secure.

He opened his eyes and looked at Denver. Denver's slashed arm hung limp at his side. Blood covered his thigh and lower leg, but his makeshift tourniquet was doing its job.

"I'm comin', man! I'm comin'!" Tony shouted. He knew he didn't have long. He grabbed the mesh again with his left hand to lessen the weight supported by his right arm. He had little left but lowered himself even with Denver. He grabbed the rope, again with both hands. He had to hold on. There would not be another casualty this day.

The two of them seemed to hang forever. Top and bottom, up and down—no longer seemed to exist.

His pain was fading, as was any feeling. Maybe they were falling after all.

If this was death, he was okay with it, as a peaceful tranquility overcame him. Something was changing.

Denver began to rise. Denver was bigger. Shouldn't he fall faster? Then the windows of the building moved passed him. Strange, he would have expected them to fly by unseen. Unknown faces stared back at him through the windows. Could his mind work that fast?

He waited for the hit. For the crush that would follow as he burst onto the ground, his organs exploding, ripping open his skin, purging his insides across the pavement. He pictured his heart rupturing, his brain mashing against the inside of his skull as the bone shattered into fragments.

"Tony ... Tony!"

Some foul, obnoxious odor filled his nose.

He wasn't moving.

He was on the ground.

He was sitting up. His back was against something hard and firm. He recognized the face in front of him.

Greg.

"Tony." Again his name.

He did not recognize the voice.

Fingers were snapping in front of his face.

His arm was being pulled, again on fire.

"You're gonna be okay," he heard someone say. It was the same voice he did not recognize. "You're gonna be okay, man."

I'm not dead, he thought.

"No you're not, buddy," said someone in a blue shirt. "You're gonna be just fine."

The world came into focus. There were others around him he didn't recognize. All were wearing blue uniforms.

He saw the sky. It was very blue. The most beautiful blue he had ever seen.

I'm in heaven.

"Close but not yet," said the paramedic leaning over him. "You're on top of Devon Tower, which sure ain't heaven."

It was then that he saw Denver lying on a stretcher. His face was white, but his eyes were open. A plastic respirator covered his mouth and nose.

"Your friend's gonna be okay."

————◆————

I'm going on my own, have to go it alone
Sorry I didn't get to say good-bye.
Tony sang into the mike. His voice carried over the PA, vibrating the walls of The Mansion—a two-thousand-seat auditorium in the west end of Toronto. They were opening for Exit—four dates on the eastern edge of their tour. Their first CD was out. Their first single—"Elizabeth's Song"—was getting airplay.

Sally smiled backstage, holding Emmy. But it wasn't Sally he was thinking about when he sang this song. Liz's memory lived on every time they played it. Sometimes he saw her face, sometimes her blonde hair, but always just out of reach.

I don't need a compass …

He sang on. He saw Liz beside him as he wrote the words on the back of the receipt. Writing with her pen, the words always close. He never had to think about them. Like his finger movements across the fret board of his bass, they were part of him.

He turned to Denver, playing lead guitar, at the second bridge of the song. They had written the music together. The bass and drums battled beats for four bars as Denver's guitar soared with a string of notes before breaking into the heavy-chorded chorus—it was an event each time they played the song, a memorial to their lost friend.

They no longer washed windows, but for a brief few minutes, Elizabeth's song brought them all back together high up on Devon Tower.

Mile Nineteen

Tom, having passed the pickup and the two young men waiting to back out onto the road, didn't give them another thought. He was getting close now—about fifteen minutes. He stopped at the next red light and waited.

He couldn't shake thinking about what he had to change in leading the team. So much of leading was about vision. It was deciding what to do and directing people to do it to create something of value. It always was and always would be. Talk could complicate and dilute it, but it didn't change its essence.

It was the lack of that vision that most affected his group. They were loaded down with their design-by-committee methods, not knowing quite where to go but going there anyway. There was no vision of what the new interface needed to be or could be. What hurt most was that Tom knew he wasn't helping. He didn't see the vision either. It was his feeling that those leading the company simply wanted to make more money that meant changing stuff. And that wasn't vision. Not only that—the value of those changes for whom the interface was intended, wasn't recognized.

It was here that things came apart for Tom and caused him the most angst. Customers—people—used the company's interfaces to control their machines, yet the human touch—or the human connection that Tom often described as "love" to raised eyebrows and rolling eyeballs—played no part in their design activities. Analysis and quantification all but ensured that, vanquishing it as if it were a weed in a garden. Any show of passion—which had overtaken him with driverlessness—was frowned upon and dismissed with contempt. It was the engineering way, the scientific method gone astray. How did they have any chance of success?

The team needed something to bring it together, something to gravitate to, to embrace as theirs. To love and feel connected to, to make real. They needed that vision.

But it's not there Tom, whispered in his head, *and you know it.*

Tom had tried, not with the company's plan but with his vision. He'd presented to the executive team. The company's interface products, that allowed people through the computer to control the machine, could play a core role in the driverless car phenomenon. The merging of technologies that was taking place—the Internet, GPS, sensor advancements—would change personal transportation forever. An impact society and the world had not seen since the automobile brought on the demise of the horse and buggy. He was relentless about how the company's technology could be the igniter of that change in personal transportation. He planted his vision whenever he could. What the product could be. He couldn't stop himself. But in the end, the discussions always came back to the company's product and cost-reduction—the minimum they could do to justify raising their price. How could they make *more* money? No one seemed concerned about what made the product worthy of an increase or what made it more valuable to customers—or to anyone for that matter. The board wasn't interested in changing the world—only filling their pockets.

Tom knew if he was honest with himself that his ideas would continue to get lost in the corporate labyrinth. They weren't a priority. The company wasn't about creating. The creating tank that fed the factory engine that drove the wheels of industry—and their company—was dry. It wasn't about to change without one person seeing, understanding, and living the need to bring the two—creating and manufacturing—together. The captain had to recognize this, decide on that vision, and lead people to it.

He picked up his cooling coffee cup. Each sip seemed to make things a little more endurable.

Without that vision, people made up their own, creating a disjointed and cumbersome chaos. Without vision, it was too easy for those not there with a love and passion for what they were doing to hide and simply do their "job." Tom saw himself as the enabler for the group to achieve a vision. To imagine, create, and build something of value like a house, a boat, or an application—or to create something new that someone didn't even know they needed. It troubled him to no end that it wasn't there.

Instead, "projects" had replaced the phenomenon of innovating. Reports and charts and Power Points had all but erased the wonderment of the glimmering "idea" and the birth of something new. Schedules and project status had usurped the magnificence of something new and original, something real, something of value. Arguments were on slide format and fonts and line spacing. The *real* reasons they were supposed to be there didn't exist anymore.

Not unlike a story with a beginning, middle, and end, they had lost their way in the deceptive middle ground. The excitement of the beginning—where the embryonic idea took form—had become lost in the midst of disinterested mediocrity. They were destined to mire in the space between the start and the finish. In the limbo of going nowhere, to eventually spiral downward until death ended it. Without a vision for something else, it was inevitable.

In Tom's thinking, what had started as a great story was not ending in failure—and a step closer to success—but worse, indifference. Everything was based on counting how many eggs were in the basket, not in finding new eggs. It was the money metric that was all-important now—that illusion of vision—leading them down the dead-end tunnel of meaninglessness. The means—the process—had become king. The process was more important than making the mirage real and, subsequently, impossible to believe in. He knew if he asked, most would refute it. Most had learned how to fake their feelings so well they no longer knew the difference. No one wanted to be revealed and show the nothingness they were working so hard to uphold. They had their own families and priorities to support. But to Tom, the evidence was clear. There really was nothing new, just talk.

It was killing him.

He sipped his coffee, hoping for reassurance.

Tom had driven past the Milton motel thousands of times, usually with only a few cars in the parking lot. Today it was a hive of police activity. He counted five black and white cruisers with more than a dozen officers milling around. His foot came off the accelerator. An ambulance was present, and a door to one of the rooms was open. Yellow police tape enclosed the area. A teenager was sitting in the back of a police cruiser with his head down.

Bad things had happened. Some kid's life was changing forever.

When he next opened his eyes, Bobby was in the caged backseat of a police cruiser. He couldn't say it was unfamiliar territory, as it wasn't his first time in the confines of a police car. His mind was numb. He didn't want to feel anything. A stretcher carrying a filled black bag slid into an ambulance. There were more uniforms than he cared to count. There was nothing he wanted to look at as a black BMW passed by on the highway. Without even seeing the driver, he hated him.

Feature No. 5—*The Polaroid Girl*

God, the car was fast. It was like flying an F-15 Eagle through the dark countryside. Dawn was still an hour off the horizon as he tore up Highway 49. The magazines were right. If the new Camaro wasn't faster than the Corvette, somebody had shit for brains. He was king, almighty and all-powerful.

Bobby blasted past a Chevy pickup as if it were parked.

It was pretty heady stuff for a sandy-haired, fifteen-year-old kid who shaved once a month. No one was going to tell him what he could or couldn't do, not a teacher and especially not his old man. And Baldwin, what the fuck did he know? It was Bobby's game to lose. The prize was his.

His arm continued to throb. He'd just become less aware of it. He touched his swollen bicep as red and white lights flashed in his rearview mirror. Things were about to get interesting. He'd been tagged.

His pulse sped up pushed on by the rush of adrenaline. His pain faded. The chase was on.

———◈———

Bobby stepped onto the crumbling concrete porch of his home. The television was on in the front room. Kelly was telling Bud to keep his pig-headed trap shut. Their screenless aluminum door creaked as he pulled it open. He didn't say a word.

"Git in here, bo'," yelled his old man as the front door slammed shut. Drunk and disorderly was what the law called it. Bobby had another name—fucking hell.

Why had he come home?

He knew what was waiting. It never changed.

Another section of the blue and yellow striped wallpaper that ran the length of the hallway was gone. It didn't matter much. It was twenty years old and overdue for replacement. Most did the stripping as part of redecorating, not because they thought life was shit and couldn't threaten someone to get them another beer. The state of the house—from the dirty dishes piled high in the sink to the scum-ringed toilets—disgusted him. They lived in a shit hole.

Stepping into the living room, he was greeted with the stench of day-old cigarette smoke, spilled beer, and foul body odor. The room was dim, lit only by the reflection of the television screen. The broken blinds were stuck closed, and torn brown curtains hung on bent curtain rods. The dimness hid the empty bottles and dirty dishes strewn around the room. His old man was sitting in his customary La-Z-Boy. The footrest was ripped. The television buzzed with an episode of *Married with Children*.

"Wuss it this time, Bobby bo'," his old man said. "F-f-feelin' up the girls again? Squeezin' their little titties? Eh, Bobby bo'."

Bobby didn't answer. The old man was not looking for an answer. It was a taunt, said only to provoke him. It was the way he spoke when he was drunk and pissed at the world—pretty much a chronic condition.

"Well, whaddya gotta say fir yerself?" the old man stammered out. He was holding the neck of a Jack Daniels bottle between his legs as if it was part of his unsavory anatomy. Beer was one thing, but Jack was a scary partner. Another empty bottle was lying on its side beside the frayed couch. Stuffing was coming through the worn-out arms like paint remover bubbling old paint off a windowsill. An empty six-pack of Pabst Blue Ribbon sat on top of the television.

"Nothin'," Bobby answered seeing the blonde ditz on the tube—such a slut. He liked that.

"School called. Said yer hasslin' … one o' the teachers."

"Didn't like what she was sayin'," Bobby answered. "Told her she could stand to lose a few fuckin' pounds."

"Watch that mouth, bo'." His old man laughed. "Wiggins, I bet."

"Yeah, the fat bitch. Needs to watch her mouth."

"When she's young, she sa foxy lady. Big fuckin' tits."

His old man was drunker than usual. JD had that effect. He only talked dirty when he was stumbling-down wasted. For a moment, he went silent like he'd forgotten where he was. Bobby hoped he'd just pass out.

"Sit down, ya little shit," he said, coming back from wherever he'd gone. "Princ'pal Smith called, said yer out. Espelled. Told 'im to shove it up 'is ass." He cackled as only a drunk can. "The fuck hung up on me."

His head came forward as if to get up.

"Gittanother JD outta the cupbert will ya," he said, pushing down on the broken footrest.

When his old man was this drunk, Bobby did as he was told. It saved having a bottle hurled at his head. He would be sleeping with his eyes open, if he stayed—which wasn't likely. There was no telling what the old man might get up to after finishing another bottle of Jack's No. 7.

He'd watched his father break his mother's arm with a baseball bat one night when he and Jack had saddled up at the kitchen table together. When he was hammered, anything that moved was a target. Television sets didn't last long either.

War and killing changed a man.

Bobby grabbed one of the four bottles in the cupboard before venturing back into the living room. As he approached the doorway, he saw the old man standing in the center of the room, resting Bobby's aluminum Eastman on his shoulder.

"Wuss-sat?" his old man sneered slurring his words together. Bobby wondered how he stood upright.

"It's the fucking Jack Daniels you wanted," Bobby replied, doing his best to show no fear.

"Wud you say?" his father shouted.

"I *said* here's your fucking Jack Daniels."

Bobby tossed the bottle toward his old man.

With the quickness of a skilled batsman, his father smashed the bottle in midair, sending the toxic liquid and shards of glass everywhere. Bobby raised his arm and turned sideways to shield himself from the blast but not before getting wet and feeling the pinpricks of broken glass against his skin. He turned back in time to see the swinging bat aimed at his head. With agility in his favor, he ducked and turned to his right. The bat punched a hole in the wall inches from his shoulder. He rolled to the ground and into the hallway, but as he stood up, a strip of pain assaulted his arm as the swinging monster connected. The blow knocked him sideways against the wall.

"You fuckin' asshole!" he screamed, doing everything he could to remain upright. If he fell, he would be pulverized by the old man's battle-axe swing.

"Ya don't talk ta me like that, ya little f-f-fuck," shouted his old man, running his words together as if spewing a long string of phlegm. "Git o'er here and take wuss comin' to ya. Take it like a fuckin' man."

Before Bobby could move again, the room exploded in a flash of light as the bat smashed into the blonde teenager on the TV. The picture tube on their secondhand RCA blew up. He was certain his old man had no idea where he was. Bobby's mission now was to get out of this hellhole—he called home—alive. This was not the first episode, but it was time to make it his last. If only he could.

"I'm gonna teach ya some fuckin' manners, bo'," his father shouted, "ya won't soon fergit."

His father's years in the police force had him instantly covering the front door in an attempt to prevent his son from escaping.

"Yer gonna pay for 'at f-f-fuckin' TV, sonny bo'," his old man snarled. "If it's the last thing ya do."

Bobby bounded up the staircase toward his bedroom two steps at a time. His heart was racing. There was no telling what the old man might get up to tonight. He was in the war zone—somewhere between Kabul and hell. Bobby's arm was screaming. He was scared shitless.

Ignoring his arm, he ran toward his room. He would jump from his second-floor bedroom window.

"Ya son of a whore!" shouted the old man from the bottom of the stairway. Through some genetic screwup, this man had fathered him into this mother of a fucked-up world. "Yuv f-f-fucked with me ... one too many times, bo'."

"Go to hell, you bastard!" shouted Bobby from the top of the stairs. "Fuck!" he screamed as he banged into the doorframe to his bedroom, setting off a whole round of new charges in his arm. "Stay the fuck away from me!"

"I'll fuckin' break you in haff ... ya don't git yer ass down here ... now!"

Bobby ran to his bedroom window. He could hear the old man slamming the bat against the staircase railing, cracking spindle after spindle as he made his way up the steps in his stupor.

Bobby was scared. If the old man caught him, he would kill him, and be all but oblivious to what he was doing. Bobby knew it like he knew his own name. He had watched the man kill Dude, the only dog they'd ever owned, on a rampage like this. It would have been him if Dude hadn't jumped up to protect him. Watching from the stairs, he'd felt the whack of every bat swing that hit the dog's sides like punches to a boxer's heavy bag. The old man had crushed the dog's head with a single two-fisted swing like cracking a shot to right center field. The bat had silenced Dude's vicious barking to little more than a raspy whimper as he dropped to the floor unconscious.

At his bedroom window, Bobby shoved the wood frame with his good arm, fully expecting it to go up. It didn't budge. For a moment, he was stunned, unable to think of what to do when his hand touched the latch on the sash. He snapped it back and pushed up as his old man barged into the room. The man seemed on skates he moved so fast. Bobby couldn't believe it. Before he could get the window up, the drop rug he was standing on was jerked out from under him. He went down on the hardwood floor like a bag of wet sand. He couldn't breathe. Pain hit like a giant spike was driven up his arm. Two feet appeared beside his head. His old man's dark shadow hovered above him.

He had but a split second. The old man was so wasted he could hardly stand up. Hesitation would have brought the bat crashing down on Bobby's skull. A quick roll sideways saved him. The bat crashed down on the hardwood floor inches from his head. Despite the hot pain in his arm, Bobby kept moving. He rolled again toward the door and crawled to his feet before his old man could raise the bat for another swing.

"Ya liddle f-f-fucker!" shouted the old man.

"Fuckin' asshole!" Bobby screamed, darting out his bedroom door. He heard the bat crash against the doorframe and drop to the floor. He ran across the landing and jumped down the stairs. The railing was a mess. Half a dozen of the wooden spindles were broken, jaggedly bent outside the neat line of the railing. The man had reached a new low. Bobby passed the destruction with one intention—to get out of the house.

He didn't touch the last four steps, leaping the distance to the bottom floor. As he ran, he listened for the sound of the Easton to crack against a wall or doorframe behind him. He ran outside and onto the porch, the outside screen door slamming against the aluminum siding unlatched as it was from its retaining chain. Not stopping or even slowing, he continued down the front steps before hearing anything from the house.

"Ah-h-h don't go, bo'. We're not done yet!" screamed the old man from the open doorway.

Bobby ran across the lawn and out to the street. He did not look back. He ran to the end of their road. Then out Taverner, along Blockner toward Main where he knew a couple of the Bulls would be hanging around outside the strip plaza on the corner. He was not going back. Not this time—no way, no how, no more.

Five of the Bulls were shuffling on the sidewalk outside Benny's Sports Bar as he made his way up Main Street. His arm throbbed. He did his best to ignore it. It was past nine and dark. The group looked restless, anxious to get another night's activities underway.

"Hey, Digs," Bobby said as he approached the group, doing his best to calm himself. "What's goin' on?"

There were a dozen cars in the parking lot. Half were parked in front of the bar. None belonged to any of the Bulls. Most of them were under age for a driver's license—not that that stopped them.

"Not much, big boy," Digs shot back. "Baldwin's still inside. Says he's got the real deal tonight."

Digs paused and slipped something red from his pocket into his mouth.

"All night long, baby."

"Yeah, whatever," Bobby replied, trying to hide his pain. "I'm in."

He rubbed his swollen right bicep that filled his hand like a grapefruit. A deep throb had replaced the flaming agony. Each time he bent it, the pain screamed for attention. He could move it. At least it wasn't broken.

"Fuck," he said, catching his breath. Ice would have helped.

"What's with the arm?" Neon smirked revealing his crooked brown teeth. Wolverine-style pork-chop sideburns he'd been growing for a few months touched the corners of his mouth. A brown, hairy tuft under his chin was part of the look. "Old man beatin' on ya again?"

Bobby didn't offer a reply. He despised giving any attention to his old man. He wanted to forget about it. Stuff the shit into that place in his head where it stayed locked up. Most of them had nothing at home. He knew Baldwin and Neon slept at A Place Somewhere most nights—a hostel for teens having a time of it at home. He'd joined them on occasion. Tonight might be another such occasion.

"What's Baldwin up to?" he asked to no one in particular.

"Tryin' to score some *al-cool-hall*," Witter replied, leaning against one of the brick columns that supported the overhang that ran the length of the plaza. Witter was the oldest gang member at seventeen. He sported a small silver ring in his eyebrow. A couple of days' prickly growth sprouted on his otherwise shaved head.

As if on cue, Baldwin pushed open Benny's entrance door. He had a brown paper bag under his arm that no doubt contained what they'd be drinking that night. Baldwin's half-brother worked the bar at Benny's and often gave him the opened bottles of wine. Being a sports bar, most patrons drank beer, but the odd one brought in their bitch that preferred a glass of wine. Most of the wine went down the drain. Giving Baldwin the opened ones helped get rid of both the wine and his little brother.

"Okay, boys," Baldwin announced in as confident a tone as any good leader could muster, "let's go down to Churchill and waste these."

Churchill was a local park where teens with nowhere else to go and little else to do hung out and got wasted.

"All right!" shouted Witter, holding a tight fist up in front of his face. "Fuckin' eh."

To Bobby, it was a choreographed scene from *The Warriors* rather than a real-life situation. Baldwin led them across the parking lot—Witter on his left, Neon on his right. Digs and Judas followed. Bobby pulled up the rear. He'd joined the gang because hanging with them made him feel cool. It felt good to be liked by Baldwin. Kind of like the older brother he never had.

"So, Ambrose, my man," Baldwin asked without turning around, "what brings you out on this fine fucking evening?"

Bobby scuffed his leather Nikes across the asphalt, not looking at anything in particular. Baldwin always called him by his last name. It was respect. The tops of his fingers were in the pockets of his Guess jeans. He tried not to think about the broken banister or his throbbing arm. The night would get better.

"Not much," he answered. Then forgetting protocol, he added, "What's goin' on tonight?"

They were not supposed to ask questions of the leader. Baldwin didn't like it. He asked the questions.

"'*What* have we got happening tonight?' the fuckin' guy wants to know," Baldwin replied in a poor imitation of Jack Nicholson.

"Well, Ambrose," he continued, "let's just say it's gonna be worth the effort."

There was more left, even at one eighty. With the agony in his arm forgotten, his foot was pressed to the floor. It was unbelievable how his speed still climbed. He had never traveled so fast in his life. He watched as the flashing lights grew distant in the rearview mirror.

The pounding beat of Guns N' Roses' "Welcome to the Jungle" pumped through him. Adrenaline danced in his bloodstream, heightened by the alcohol and Adderall he'd consumed in the park. Didn't that beat all? Fuckin' right it did. Nothing could touch him. Not man or machine. The zone was his and his alone.

His eyes stayed glued to the roadway as the wheels of the Camaro gobbled up the pavement beneath him.

The night's conquest Baldwin had titled "Get the Babe". The first one to Milton—a three-hour drive from Alstown—got the girl he had holed up in a motel. The girl was important—Bobby hadn't had a bitch in two weeks—but the winner earned respect points. He wasn't about to disappoint Baldwin. That wasn't going to happen. He had worked hard to get in. Had cost him a friend and part of a finger. He knew Milton. He had the advantage. There could be no fuckups.

"Do what you want, but fucking bring her back," were Baldwin's only instructions.

Shortly after three o'clock in the morning, the four of them had lined up across from Warner's Pontiac-Buick dealership. They all were to get cars. Digs, the Bulls' lock specialist, would break into the showroom office and throw out four sets of keys—a set for each of them: Witter, Judas, Neon, and Bobby.

Before they started, Baldwin had held up a Polaroid of the girl. Bobby figured she looked about his age, with long, blonde hair that hung down the sides of her China-doll face. Silver mascara and black lashes magnetized her dark eyes. Her black painted-lip smile revealed straight white teeth. A diamond sparkled on the side of her nose. In the picture, she wore a white halter-top with thin straps over her shoulders. Bobby had noticed the outline of her dark nipples through the stretched fabric. The photo served to crank up further what a combination of raging teenage hormones and drugs and alcohol in the park had already initiated. He was hard and ready to burst.

They had watched Digs break in. Baldwin had given the signal. With his index finger, he'd pointed at the dealership like he was firing a gun. They ran across the street as Digs threw the keys onto the paved lot out front. Neon was first to the keys, but instead of picking up a set and frantically searching for the car they belonged to, he had grabbed three sets and thrown them toward the garbage bin beside the service garage. Witter and Judas had followed the keys like fetching dogs. Bobby being closer, his arm still screaming, was having none of it.

Neon could outrun him—he was first to the keys—but Bobby had him by twenty pounds. He didn't hesitate. He could have made first-string defensive end on the Alstown High football team with the sack he put on his fellow Bull. With his elbows raised, he had hit Neon just below the solar plexus, sending them both to the curb in front of the dealership.

Bobby paid little attention to the fallen Neon or the other Bulls. He picked up the fallen keys and in less than a minute matched the license number on the key fob to a midnight-black Chevy Camaro.

It was a magnificent machine. Only in his dreams had he experienced such a car. He forgot about his old man at the house. There was little doubt in his mind that the babe in the Polaroid would be his for the taking.

He slipped onto the leather seat and shoved the key in the ignition. The engine fired to life with a hungry growl. Smiling, he gripped the black leather-wound steering wheel like he owned the world. Nothing could get in his way. He was unstoppable. The car rumbled, shaking him in the driver's seat as he reversed out of the parking spot. Pulling in front of the dealership, tugged by the awesome horsepower, he saw Neon still on the ground. He wasn't moving. Digs stood beside him and shot Bobby the finger.

Bobby responded by stomping on the accelerator. The massive engine torque unglued the rear tires from the pavement, almost sending him into the wall of the dealership. He fought the steering wheel to get the bucking machine under control. Screeching out of the lot, he spewed stone and asphalt over Digs and the fallen Neon, leaving the putrid smell of burned rubber assaulting the air.

Baldwin was standing on the other side of the road. For an instant, their eyes met. Baldwin held up the Polaroid and nodded. For the first time, Bobby had felt on common ground with the Bulls' leader.

The red flashing lights filled his rearview mirror. Alice in Chains was cranked beyond the sound barrier. He barely could hear himself think. Nothing beyond the pounding reverberation of "Rooster" got through. The needle on the speedometer touched two hundred. The road disappeared beneath the long hood of the car at an alarming rate. The dashed centerline became a blur. Gobs of horsepower were under his right foot. He was in charge and above the law—untouchable.

I can do this, he thought, glimpsing the flashing lights on the police car in his side mirror. His rear view was filled with the blasting strobe lights on the cruiser's roof. The night was lit up like he was trying to outrun a raging forest fire with tongues of red heat licking at his heels.

The cruiser was losing ground. He'd held off two cars for half an hour already.

Closing in on Milton, dawn was on the horizon. He knew where he had to go.

He did not let up. The flashing lights stayed with him. He didn't look at the speedometer. He glimpsed at a sign for Milton. He would take the first exit.

The photograph of the girl came into his head. He wanted her. No one else was going to get there first. He wasn't about to give them a chance.

His foot stayed hard to the floor. The highway was straight. The roadside signs were ghastly outcroppings in the conical beams of the Camaro's headlights. The exit appeared. He was hard onto the brakes. A cruiser was on his back bumper. He watched it fishtail in his mirrors. Alice in Chains still pounded his eardrums. Scared, he had difficulty holding to the tight curve. The front tires ploughed forward—only inches from the gravel marbles of the shoulder that threatened to carry him off the road and end his game—before grabbing and sending him around the ramp as if on rails.

The incessant flashing lights continued to bear down on him like a bloodhound chasing a rabbit through the forest. They wanted his ass. He was in big shit if they caught him.

The traffic light was red at the end of the ramp, but Bobby wasn't stopping. He tore through the intersection as the rear end twitched sideways. Turning the steering wheel into the slide, he righted the over steer and then trounced down on the accelerator. With the momentum of a slingshot, he flew down the road through several intersections before turning left on another red. He was close.

With the sky lightening, Bobby took no notice.

Storefronts, houses, gas stations flew past on both sides. Things looked familiar. He had lived here as a child with memories best left forgotten. A map wasn't necessary to find the Skylark Motel where Baldwin had the girl holed up.

On his left, not far ahead, appeared the motel's lighted neon sign. The place looked old and shabby from what he remembered. The L was missing from the motel's sign. "Sky ark" was how it read. He sped by. Driving in now would finish him. He had to lose the law first.

It was still early, so there was little traffic to contend with. He led the pursuit of flashing lights toward the east end of town. About a mile beyond the motel, he braked hard and turned left into an unknown subdivision. He heard the screeching tires above the driving beat of Ozzie's "Crazy Train". He doubled the speed limit and, in his rearview mirror, watched the cruiser closest to him blow out a front tire bucking a curb.

"Fuckin' eh!" he screamed and slammed the steering wheel with his fist, reigniting the pain in his arm.

Without hesitating, he turned left again at the first street he came to. He punched the brake pedal and was back on the accelerator as the front driver-side tire brushed the curb. Undeterred, he jostled the steering wheel back and forth to gain control. He had all but committed to taking the next right when at the last moment he saw the sign *Greenfield Crescent*, an easy roadblock for his pursuers that would end his race—and his freedom. A twitch of the steering wheel kept him straight. He was at the next street before the cruiser made the turn behind him. The space was growing between them. Again, he turned left. This time too sharply and bounced off the inside curb. The rear end came loose. Forced wide, he came close to losing control but caught the slide with a lucky jerk of the steering wheel. On reflex, his foot found the brake. The four wheels locked up. It was enough to miss the opposite curb. He didn't wait and tromped on the throttle. The rear wheels spun like a polar bear clawing for grip on an ice flow. Loose gravel and stones flung from the tires. The pungent smell of burned rubber soiled the air as the wide, rear tires finally took hold to send him forward. Accelerating, he made a sharp right only to slide on the opposite side. He did not let off the gas this time. With adrenaline forcing his head forward—his chin all but touching the steering wheel—he sped onward.

The incessant flashing lights that had filled his rearview mirror faded into dimmed reflections off the fronts of neighboring houses. The law was backing off? His eyes scanned the neighborhood for his next means of escape—a driveway, a pathway, even a park. The throbbing drums of Metallica provided the soundtrack. *Sleep with one eye open* ... bellowed through the speakers, pumping Bobby beyond any thrill ride he had ever experienced.

His amphetamine-alert eyes saw two vans parked in single file in a double driveway on his left. His decision was instant. It was time to bug out.

He tromped on the brake pedal. The car slid sideways, the right rear coming forward as if trying to catch the right front, the reverse of a dog chasing its tail. He was living Steve McQueen's *Bullitt*. The slide helped him negotiate the turn. The right front tire bumped the curb as he shot up into the driveway almost to the garage door.

The Camaro hadn't stopped moving when he slammed the floor shift into park and pushed the door open. A hundred decibels of Metallica assaulted the early-morning quiet of the suburban neighborhood through the open car door. With little wherewithal, he reached back in and turned off the car. It was then he heard the screaming police sirens. This was real. He froze, scared shitless. His arm throbbed back to life. No juvie for him; he'd be going to jail if they caught him.

The image of the girl in the Polaroid returned. He started moving.

He pushed off the car door, closing it. The large, two-story house looked new and expensive. Using the vans for cover, he crossed the front yard and ran through a flowerbed and shrubs. A quick look back as he rounded the side of the brick house revealed two cruisers already on the street. They were not slowing; tires and sirens screamed. The vans would give him a few seconds. He hoped it was enough. They would never catch him on foot. Of that he was certain. He was running for his life; they were doing their jobs.

He vaulted over a wood fence at the side of the house and landed in the thick, overgrown grass of the next yard.

God damn people, he could hear his old man saying about the homeowners, *don't fuckin' deserve what they got!*

Shrieks of locked-up tires on the pavement overpowered the sirens. They'd spotted the Camaro.

He ran the full length of the backyard, passing a wood-frame jungle gym, a park-size sandbox, and an aluminum tool shed. Going over their back fence, he dropped into the waist-high grass of the field that sided the subdivision and kept running. The length of grass slowed his progress but at the same time helped conceal him.

He didn't look back. The line of fences separating the domesticated lawns from the acres of untended field became his path. When he reached the end of the subdivision, his whole body was heaving. His injured arm was on fire. Each step seemed to send an agonizing bolt of lightning to his brain. His hammering heartbeat filled his ears. Gasping, there was no time to stop. He had to get back to the highway.

He hopped a four-foot chain-link fence and started across the backyard of a corner lot. He was committed before he saw the giant Great Dane come down from the side of the house. The dog snarled, baring a jagged row of teeth at the unwanted intruder. He didn't hesitate and kept his legs pumping. He was over the fence before the dog started to bark, praying it would shut up.

He kept running. The lights of the "Sky ark" came into view. Another half mile, and he would collect his prize.

Out of breath, his thighs burned, and his arm ached. He ran like he'd never run before. His whole body told him to stop. *You've lost them*, he told himself. *It's okay, you're gonna make it.* He dropped to the bottom of the drainage ditch that ran beside the highway. His legs kept him moving as he stayed low in the ditch for cover. He didn't hear the sirens. In the distance, he could hear tires lighting up the pavement, but no one was chasing behind him. As he struggled through the ditch, he saw the occasional passing car, but that was all. The sun was slowly creeping over the horizon. The protection of the dark was gone.

You can do it, man, you can do it, kept repeating in his head as he moved in ankle-deep water at the bottom of the ditch.

The Polaroid had the number 14 written on the back. The key was supposed to be under the mat in front of the door.

Bobby stopped at the cement culvert beside the motel and turned around. The sirens may have faded but the flashing lights were evident in the distance. Cruisers were moving through the subdivision labyrinth. They weren't about to give up.

Lacking any sort of plan, Bobby scrambled up the bank of the ditch. As calmly as he could manage, wearing sopping-wet Nikes, he walked across the paved parking lot. If anybody approached, he was part of the maintenance crew. *Three mornings a week, I clean up guest garbage before school*, he thought to himself. It wasn't much of a story.

As he crossed the lot, he watched the room numbers descend. He headed toward the door marked number 14. A brown Ford F150 pickup and a white Buick were parked in front of the rooms adjacent to it. The drapes were pulled across the large front window.

A black doormat lay in front of each gray door.

He stopped at the door with 14 on it. Without hesitating, he bent down and lifted the corner of the mat.

He smiled. Dirt, stones, a Mars bar wrapper, and a pink piece of dried-up gum surrounded the dirty brass key.

He'd made it. He'd won.

He inserted the key and turned the doorknob. The door opened easily. It was only then he thought of knocking.

It was dark inside. The only light came through the open door. He paused to let his eyes adjust. There didn't seem to be anyone there. Still unable to see but afraid of being seen, he stepped inside and closed the door.

He waited and listened. Listened for sounds—for breathing, for presence, for anything. There was no one there.

The nauseous reek of days-old McDonalds and spilled beer hit his nose. It seemed to embody everything he'd been through and the shit he was in.

Was it all a setup? There was no one else even close.

He stayed still. They may not be here now, but someone had been here. Slowly, edges and surfaces made themselves visible. A bed, another door, and the dark rectangle of a television set.

He could feel his heart slamming inside his chest and the mad pulse of blood pumping through his neck. His arm was alive and throbbing.

He couldn't see anyone, but he didn't feel alone.

Remaining hopeful that his prize was there somewhere, his hand found the wall switch. A corner floor lamp cast light across the room.

Bobby had imagined finding the girl in the Polaroid sprawled on the bed. His teenage brain had conjured up all kinds of twisted scenarios. From finding her spread-eagled with her ankles and wrists bound to the bedposts to quietly sleeping under the laundered-stiff motel sheets. In his head, she was always naked and expectant of his arrival.

But what appeared before him in the less than bright room was an empty bed with the covers pulled down like someone had gotten up to visit the can in the middle of the night and stayed there.

"Fuck!" he cursed, thinking about what he'd gone through to arrive at an empty motel room. His injured arm renewed its vigor. If he were caught, he would be spending time at Hutton, the detention center out on Highway 5 for sure. Maybe even behind bars. He had so anticipated getting laid. Anger pumped him with the sudden urge to jerk off in the bed.

"Aahhmmm."

A muffled sound came from behind the other door that had to be the bathroom. It was unmistakable. Someone was in there. Fear replaced his anxiousness. *What had he walked into?*

His eyes went to the beer bottles littering the brown carpet. He relaxed. She was drunk. Likely puking in the toilet. What a prize.

"Fuck!" he cursed again, slamming his palm against the cinderblock wall beside the door he'd closed. Instant pain shot across his hand. It sharpened his thinking. He reached for the doorknob. Time to go. There was no way he was going to get caught in this mess.

"Aaarrrmm."

Another, louder groan came from behind the other door.

He stopped and thought for a moment. He had no place to go. It seemed foolish at this point to chance exposure to the ones he had worked so hard to elude.

Mad, frustrated, and ready to take his shit-for-luck out on somebody else, he turned away from the door and crossed the room. He touched the bathroom door's metal doorknob. It felt cool beneath his fingers. The knob wouldn't turn. The door was locked.

"Open the door," he said into the doorjamb. Shouts in a motel room at six o'clock in the morning would bring unwanted attention.

"Aahh! ... Ahh!" he heard from behind the door. He stopped. A chill crept up the back of his neck.

Without thinking, he spoke the obvious.

"It's locked."

No answer.

A flash of panic went off in his head. He had outmaneuvered the police in an impossible chase only to end up in a motel room with a stranger locked behind a bathroom door unable or unwilling to speak. He pictured himself busted for stealing the car and reckless driving but never for human trafficking. He didn't know what Baldwin was into, but he was pretty sure it wasn't legal. He was fried. He had nowhere to go. He could leave, but to what end?

He looked at the door.

This was not the first time he'd faced a locked bathroom door. In the past, he was the one on other side.

He gripped the steel knob with both hands and tried to turn it. It didn't move. Squatting, he noticed the tiny hole in the center of the round knob. He had his way in.

The drawers in the television stand yielded nothing. The drawer in the small nightstand had a white ballpoint with "Skylark" stenciled in green across the side. He had what he needed. His nimble fingers twisted the pen apart and pulled out the steel insert. Perfect. MacGyver had nothing on him.

He slid the metal insert through the hole in the knob. A push. A click. He was in.

He turned the knob and pushed the door. A smear of blood on the gray floor tiles stopped him. *Shit!* Again, the urge to flee tempted him. This was fucking bullshit. He was going to get fried, sure as Chucky had cheese.

He might get away if he left now, but the open exposure of the only door out held him in place. Getting away once was lucky. Trying to escape a second time was suicide. If any luck were to side with him, staying put was his best bet. Winning the prize was over.

He pressed forward. There was a chance—a sliver of hope—but still hope.

He pushed the door further. More blood. *Fuck!* The front of the toilet came into view. Blood streaks ran down the side.

Sickness came upon him like leeches on live flesh. His stomach did a sickening flip. The urge to heave chilled him.

He tried to stop and not see any more. But he'd gone too far.

Something behind the door resisted his push. He saw the side of the bathtub. Trails of blood ran to the floor.

"Ahm … aahhmm …" The unknown voice grew louder.

Bobby pushed the door harder, revealing even more blood on the floor and the towels blocking the door.

Sight of her feet came first—black painted toenails like the fingernails in the photo. He'd found the Polaroid girl. Something turned inside him, something he didn't understand. Against a strong desire to bolt, he moved closer. She needed more help than he did.

Her skin was as white as the tub's enamel. A lone, unpainted toenail was purple, almost matching the others. Gray duct tape bound her ankles together. His eyes ran along her blood-streaked legs. He pushed the door further. He was not prepared for what he saw.

Her eyes were wide and bulging in their sockets. It almost seemed worse that she was alive. Horror struck with the realization a person was behind the deadness that stared back at him. Her eyes showed a cold darkness he'd not seen in a person before. He thought it was fear but realized it was much deeper than that. He saw hopelessness. She was shaking, cowering.

Blood was everywhere. In the tub, on her arms and face, sprinkled like raindrops in her bleached blonde hair and on the tiled walls surrounding the bathtub. Her forearms and biceps were open gashes. Her forehead was slashed. Her wrists were tied to the bloodied chrome assistance rail. More duct tape was wrapped around her head, sealing her mouth. She was too weak to move. Her eyes revealed a terror unknown to Bobby. He could not imagine what she had been through.

"Ahmm ..." She tried to speak, too confused to know what to make of him.

He dropped to his knees and leaned over the edge of the tub. She recoiled. Her entire body shuddered in expectation of more violence to what already had been inflicted on her.

"It's okay, it's okay," he repeated softly in an attempt to console her. His own voice quivered. At once she seemed lucid yet in the next instant gone, as her head sagged to one side.

Precious seconds ticked by. For a moment, he thought she was dead. He reached out and touched her arm. She jumped as if his hand was charged with electricity. He pulled back. Though restricted by the duct tape, she still tried to draw away. Ragged fear filled her eyes. She was terrified. It scared him.

"It's okay," he whispered. "I'm here to help you."

His words seemed to reassure her. Or was it just him? Her body seemed to relax while her eyes remained wide and wary.

He held his hands open in front of her.

"I won't ..." he whispered, his voice trembling, "I won't hurt you."

He reached for the end of the tape that stood out like a flap of skin at the side of her head. She'd been bound and gagged in a hurry. What other violence had been played out on her? He didn't want to imagine. It hurt to think. Her head turned sharply as he touched the tape.

"It's cool, girl," he whispered, pulling his hand away, "Let me get this shit off you."

The tape-over-tape came off easily, but she snapped her head viciously when the tape pulled her skin. Her gagged voice raised in pitch. She jerked away, making it difficult to continue. Gripping the tape firmly, he gave it a hard tug and tore it from her mouth. A sock stuffed in her mouth came with it.

"Aahhrgg," was all she could manage, weeping and then going limp. A moment later, she turned away, forcing her face against the tiled wall.

"I'll get you out," he whispered.

His hands went to her ankles and again pulled off the tape. He worked fast.

"Owww," she groaned, trying to pull her legs away from his hands. She had a small child's strength. She began to sob. Bobby wondered whether she even knew where she was as he pulled off the tape.

She had lost a lot of blood. The crimson disturbed her stark whiteness.

"I'm … sorry … Jim … my," she mumbled.

His hands went to her side. Her skin was cold and goose-fleshed like the skin of a plucked chicken. She did not flinch this time or even try to move. He could not help notice her naked chest. Her nipples purple, sitting on her white skin like small blueberries. Blood from the gash on her shoulder ran between them.

He slid his hands underneath her body to pick her up. She was as light as a young child—amazingly thin. He set her back down. Without knowledge of first aid, his instinct was to get her warm. She needed care. He could provide it.

His eyes went to the blood-splotched dark hair between her legs. The prize he had come for now forgotten.

But the blood. So much blood. Spread across her legs. Across her arms. Across her face. Between her legs, discoloring the curls—dark, crimson, and violent. It ran down the sides of the white bathtub. Down the steel drain. Away from her ravaged body.

He grabbed two towels and covered her as best he could.

"It's gonna be okay," he whispered close to her face.

Then he slid his arms under her again and stood up. Turning as best he could in the small space, he was careful not to knock her feet or head against the door or doorframe.

"Ah … please …" she uttered as her head lulled backward against his arm. He stepped back inside the room.

Someone knocked at the door.

He stopped in disbelief.

"This is the police! Open the door!"

He stood holding the dying girl, remembering what he'd done.

"Open the door! We know you're in there!"

The words were like electric shocks to his head. Was it simply a matter of time before they caught up with him?

"She needs a hospital!" he shouted. His voice was hoarse, not his own. His mind was racing. He could save her life or try to save his own.

He carried her to the door, bent slightly, and turned the doorknob. The door opened far enough for him to get his foot in, still holding the girl in his arms.

"Please!" he cried stepping into the doorway.

Outside, a cop was positioned on the left side of door. Two more were on his right. All of them had their guns drawn and pointed at his chest. Ready to drop him. Another cop was leaned over the trunk of a cruiser parked directly in front of the room. He had a rifle pointed at Bobby—the hunted prey.

"She needs a doctor!" Bobby shouted, his voice cracking. He was in big shit, but she was going to die. He didn't even know her name.

"Put her down on the sidewalk real slow and get on the ground," the lone cop on his left said sternly. "Slow, son, real slow."

Bobby bent down as directed—slowly. He laid his dying Polaroid girl on the pavement as gently as he could. She wasn't moving.

Her blood coagulated on his skin. It had soaked through his shirt and covered his hands. He slipped his arms out from under her. He couldn't feel her breathing. When he looked up, he saw the car.

"Easy, son, nice and easy."

Her body was limp. Her head didn't move. Her eyes were closed.

"She needs a doctor!" Bobby pleaded, his voice trembling as he spoke.

"On the ground!" shouted the officer "Help's on its way. Get the fuck down."

Bobby eased himself to the asphalt.

"You're under arrest for—" a cop behind him started to say.

"She's gonna die!" he screamed as a cop kneed him in the back, pinning him to the ground, grinding his cheek into the rough pavement.

His wrists were cuffed together. His arm lit up. Time disappeared. As he was jerked to his feet, he saw them. Baldwin was standing beside a car near the motel entrance. Someone else was inside the car. It was then he knew. The cops hadn't found him at all.

In the instant it took to figure it out, one of the officers on his right grabbed his injured arm and jerked him sideways. The pain all but dropped him to his knees.

"Stand up, you little prick," spat the forceful cop, any formality nonexistent. "Move!"

Bobby was slammed against the right front fender of the patrol car parked in front of the room he'd carried the girl from.

"It's the last time I'm getting dragged across hell's half acre by a fucked-up kid."

The words meant nothing to Bobby. He felt the same hopelessness he'd seen in the eyes of his Polaroid girl.

While leaned over the hood of the cruiser, a nightstick cracked against the back of his right hamstring. He closed his eyes. The stick was then cranked up between his legs and mashed into his balls, curdling his stomach. As he slid off the hood, another officer kneed him in his left thigh. He was no longer human but a bag of shit to be kicked around. Someone grabbed a fist full of his sandy hair and pushed his face into the cruiser's fender. The next thing he knew he was on the ground, staring at the small, gray stones stuck in the tire treads of the cruiser.

Two hard-toed boot kicks hit him in the side, cracking two ribs, the pain numbing his body. His eyes closed. His father's face flashed in front of him.

"You have the right to speak to a lawyer …"

Bobby heard the word "lawyer" but that was all. His body rose through no effort of his own. His forehead hit the side of the cruiser's doorframe.

"Ah, fuck!" shouted an officer somewhere behind him. "She's not breathing, Captain!"

"Game's fuckin' over, kid," growled a voice above him, "for this life."

An elbow came down on the side of his face, cracking his cheekbone as he fell into the back of the cruiser.

Blackness swamped him. He didn't hear another thing.

Mile Twenty-Five

Tom sat waiting on the red light. Seeing the commotion in the motel's parking lot did not sit well with him. It was real and disturbing. A kid was in big trouble and likely going to jail.

Another few lights and a stretch of highway would have him turning into the company parking lot. When the light turned green, instead of going straight, he turned right. He didn't feel like driving into work quite yet. He needed more time to digest what he'd seen and get himself reoriented.

There was still coffee in his cup. He drank it. The creamy sweetness left a sour taste in his mouth.

His stomach turned raw with the thought of facing the executive team later that day. It wasn't nerves so much as would they hear him this time? His prototype car and business plan were solid. He'd reasoned and agonized over them ad infinitum. He was ready. The idea was too important to miss. His video of the remote-control car, he had to admit, was brilliant. Proof that the concept was real and worked. What lay ahead of them was magnificent. The board had to see the possibilities this time.

At the next left, he turned. He hadn't taken this route in months, maybe even a year. He made his way along the road that, after a number of winding turns, brought him back to the route he would have otherwise been on. He came to the old, red brick house he would have passed coming from the other direction. The large garage that sided the house made the century home look oddly different. It was all but unseen from the main thoroughfare through town. For an instant, he wondered whether he'd taken the right turn, unaccustomed to the view from this angle. But at the stop sign in front of the corner lot, he recognized the area. He turned right back to his regular route in.

He wasn't thirty seconds on the highway when flashing lights appeared in his rearview mirror. His heart shot to his throat as it always did when the lights of a police car lit up his mirrors. Damn, a speeding ticket. Checking his speedometer, he wasn't over the limit. Then he saw the red taillights.

There were two cars ahead of him. One was slowing. The other was off the road on the other side of a long, uprooted chunk of otherwise neatly trimmed hedge. It no longer resembled a car but instead a mass of mangled automobile crushed against an immovable cement abutment. Something had gone horribly wrong in the minutes preceding his approach.

Tom wasn't aware he'd brought the BMW to a stop. Nor was he aware of springing from the car and leaving it running.

He was surprised by how much the scene looked like something he'd seen before. The puddle under the front of the deformed car—black and round—was like any other puddle really. It might have been blood were it a movie. Yes, in fact, that's how it felt—like a movie set—surreal and staged, not real. A woman, whom he didn't recognize, was talking, babbling, pleading with him to help her like he was a close friend. The wreckage had happened in mere seconds—minutes before he'd stopped the BMW—but the devastation would never be forgotten.

There was a gash across the woman's forehead. Blood covered her left eye and streamed down the left side of her thin, pretty neck. She was holding a beautiful mauve scarf, one she'd likely put on while staring back at herself in the long mirror in the front foyer of her home, just before putting her arm in the sleeve of her no-longer-white waist jacket. The one with large, white buttons done up almost to her now brilliant red neck.

"Please help me," she begged, spraying red spittle as she spoke. A beautiful, blue eye as large as a baseball stared back at him or at something. "I'm going to be late for work."

Tom reached forward, dumbfounded by what he was seeing, and accepted her hand. The warm softness was alarming, so in contrast to the destruction all around them. Her grip was firm but soft. He stared at her hand.

"Tell Jenny ... it'll be okay ..."

The woman spoke in little more than a whisper. Seeing the brilliant redness on the stark whiteness of her coat startled Tom. The intensity thrust what he saw into crystal clarity.

The woman's blue eye looked into his.

"Please tell Jenny ..." she whispered again.

Her lip quivered. Her grip tightened then diminished. Her eye didn't move.

Tom didn't know what to do other than keep holding her hand when another hand squeezed his shoulder.

"Sir, I'll take her from here."

It was an official-sounding voice that spoke and triggered something in Tom to make the scene real. The uniformed professional was precise and efficient in his movements, maneuvering in between Tom and the injured woman.

"You're going to be okay," said the paramedic to the woman. "We'll just get you outta here and ..."

"She's gonna be okay ..." Tom interrupted as much to himself as to the paramedic. It was a question in his mind spoken as a wavering statement.

"Excuse me, sir," said a woman in another uniform. Her hand touched Tom's arm. "You okay?"

He nodded and repeated, "Yeah, she's gonna be okay ..."

"Alec'll take good care of her," the young woman said in a kind but practiced tone. "She's in the best of hands."

After giving his contact information and a brief statement about what little he'd witnessed, Tom walked back to his BMW. His keys weren't in his pocket. They were on the seat. Odd, he didn't remember leaving them there, but he didn't remember leaving the car either.

He looked at the dashboard clock. Half an hour had passed.

Restarting the BMW, he drove around the parked emergency vehicles and merged back into the growing traffic.

——◆◈◆——

Jason noticed the black BMW parked at the side of the road. He'd been writing for about an hour when he stood up from his seat in front of his Mac. He'd been thinking about how much his life had changed in the past year while looking around his large workroom with the picture window that faced the street. He might have heard a siren but couldn't be sure. It hadn't alarmed him enough to pull him from his work. Sirens in town weren't that unusual. Seeing the BMW wasn't that remarkable, but the flash of emergency vehicles' lights certainly was.

At first, he couldn't see the cause of the disturbance because of the narrow stretch of Parsons Park that separated their street from the main highway. A large chunk of hedge was missing as if cleared out by a backhoe. Like sunlight twinkling through the leaves of the maple trees that marked the park's periphery came the flash of lights from police cars, fire trucks, and two ambulances. An array of uniformed officials was in action.

Then he saw it.

The shocking destruction was made more astounding by its proximity and the fact that he hadn't been aware it had even happened. He saw the savage devastation that only man-gone-wrong with manmade contrivances can manifest. It destroyed people's lives. A car had hit the cement abutment that supported the monument to one of Stanton's founders.

Jason was about to sit back down when a man walking toward the BMW caught his eye. The man was wearing a blue, short-sleeved dress shirt and gray slacks. Balding, his head was down. Jason guessed the man had witnessed the accident and was quite shaken by it. He intuited a story taking seed. The man gave Jason pause to reflect on his own life.

He watched the man open the driver's side door and reach in to retrieve something from the seat before climbing in.

The car then maneuvered slowly around a police car to merge into the passing traffic and the rest of the world.

Feature No. 6—*Saved by 532*

Bzzzzzz!

The buzzer went off beside his head like a fire alarm. His hand shot out to shut the damn thing off. The obnoxious plastic box would have the whole house awake.

On his night table, the clock read 4:20 a.m. Unbelievable.

He slid out from his cocoon of warm blankets and sat on the edge of the bed. Denise didn't move. He used to wake with an urging erection but not anymore. She wouldn't notice he was gone until seven thirty or so when she would rise, barely coherent, and get Jack and Lynn ready for school.

Standing up, his left heel sparked with pain. Over the winter, he'd succumbed to what his doctor called plantar fasciitis—a common running injury. He was supposed to stay off it—like he had time. With his home and work schedules as they were, he would just have to suck up a Latin foot condition. It would have to get better on its own. He shuffled past his clothes dresser to the bathroom. Brush, floss, shave, and shower.

In the dark, he pulled on a fresh, white, cotton dress shirt to go with his gold tie and new olive Tommy Hilfiger suit. Today his team was traveling to Chicago to visit a supplier, so he had to step up his regular wardrobe of trousers and a golf shirt. Dressing up changed his usual routine and outlook. There was something special about the crispness of a pressed dress shirt, like the smell of brewing coffee. It made him feel better.

Dressed, he stepped in his closet, closed the door, and turned on the light so as not to disturb Denise. In the mirror on the back of the closet door, he had to admit he looked sharp and very professional. He turned to leave when his eyes caught sight of the cardboard carton on the shelf above his hanging clothes. The box contained the stories he'd written over the years and never published. *What could have been*, he thought and then switched off the light and left.

By five o'clock that morning, he was ready and anxious to leave. His taxi to the airport had not yet arrived.

The first edition of the *Toronto Star*, with its familiar blue logo reminding him of his beloved Maple Leafs, was on the front doorstep. Checking his watch, he wondered what hour the kid who delivered the paper got up. The front-page headline read "FAA Hails New Safety Regs." That was good news. Were they *unsafe* before? He looked at his watch. Where was the damn taxi? Stanton wasn't that far out in the boonies. For a second, he wondered whether Sarah had remembered to arrange one. Moments later, as he pulled out the sports section, lights from a car pulling into their driveway shone across their living room wall.

Alone in the cover of darkness, he left his sleeping household to embark upon another business trip to the great U.S. of A.

The morning went well, better than expected.

The flight was on time. His assistant, Sarah White, and senior procurement officer, Darryl Hawthorn, were too. Their supplier was ready for the visit. Committed deliveries. Pricing review. Quality metrics. New products. All organized and well prepared and yet—so boring. If he had been through one, he had been through fifty vendor visits—same thing, again and again with different people. As was protocol, he complimented the group on their preparation and fine presentation. They managed to finish just before one in the afternoon.

Lunch was as relaxed as business lunches got. For a change, they did not talk shop, but everyone remained within their windows of professionalism. He was never entirely comfortable in this setting; too many watchful eyes checking postures and gestures, movements, tones, and inflections. They put meaning where there was no intent and intent when there wasn't any. Being the most significant company representative, he was the leader and held the most responsibility and, likewise, attention. When he leaned forward, everyone followed suit. He ordered soda, so everyone ordered something nonalcoholic. He selected a turkey club sandwich, and the others followed by ordering something of similar price. It was just the way things worked, and they were not about to change.

Standard fare was to talk about the weather. It was Jason's first indicator of a group's awkwardness and preference for small talk over the possible conflict of discussing anything meaningful. The anxiety of silence was worse and to be avoided like a contagion. It was incredible how interested people could appear to be in talking about the weather under such forced circumstances. Sports usually followed. An equally inane subject he had grown tired of but gobbled up more conversation time. He was glad he'd browsed the sports section earlier so he could at least participate with some level of knowledge. The weather impacted a person's life much more than sports. Yet sports had a way of bringing passion and emotion out in people that would otherwise lie dormant. People liked to get excited about things that really had no discernible effect on their lives. That was small talk and a routine that was not Jason's forte but an understood part of the job. Anyone could learn to adapt.

Then from out of the blue came the thought—how in the world had he ended up at this dead-end place going nowhere—that coincided with the next point of conversation.

"Here's a story that got me," Jake, the supplier's operations manager, interjected, causing a couple of heads to turn. Excused from the earlier meetings, he had joined them for lunch. He hadn't said much, looking more than a little bored.

"My neighbor, a young guy about your age," he nodded at Jason, "disappeared last week. Just vanished. Left a wife and three small kids."

"Really," Jason replied, moved by the abrupt change in subject matter. He sipped his soda.

"Men." Sarah sighed, shaking her head. Just two years out of college, what she lacked in experience she more than made up for with ambition and spunk. She wouldn't be around long. Her sights were set on far bigger things.

"Yeah, like it's only men," Darryl retorted, giving her the gears. He and his wife had a new baby at home. In suffering the effects of sleep deprivation, he often stumbled into Sarah's web like a disoriented fly.

Jason drifted out of the conversation. His early morning was catching up with him, causing his mind to wander. He was intrigued by the story of the disappearing family man. It gave possibility to his dead end of going nowhere. But disappearing was way out there. Could someone just walk away from their life and be gone? Was it guts that separated those who did from those who only thought about it?

"A woman is at least up-front and direct."

Sarah's voice brought him back to the conversation. She was getting in her last dig. Chairs were shifting, and cups were emptying. It was time to wrap up.

Could a person really vanish? He found himself unable to let go of the idea as they made their way back to the airport. Could you actually disappear and begin another life? Strange thoughts for a family man considered "happy" with his life? Or was that the point?

Imagine no more responsibility. No more showing up for work. No more trying to please everyone. Just start over—clean slate. Maybe even get it right this time.

His brain paused on Denise as they entered the departures area at O'Hare. He would send money anonymously. Let her create a better life for all of them, maybe even be happy. Waiting in line for his gate pass, he convinced himself Denise would adjust. She was tough and determined.

Then it hit—overtook him in an avalanche of spontaneity. He *could* disappear. No plan, no analysis, just *be gone*.

One decision. One action.

Standing in line, he glanced at Darryl chatting up the blonde attendant at the counter. Darryl wouldn't notice him leaving. Turning, he saw Sarah on her cell, likely checking voicemail. She wouldn't notice either. Both were absorbed.

Go. Now!

His pulse quickened. He turned and looked up at the Departures Level sign beside the entrance they had come through. He glanced again at Sarah and Darryl, and then checked his watch. Beads of sweat were on his forehead. Both anxious and hesitant, he stepped sideways out of the queue. His feet seemed to move by themselves.

For an instant, he again questioned what he was doing. But he kept moving. There was an ATM on his right. Cash would give him time to cover his trail and not give away anything, as Denise knew he was in Chicago. His maximum withdrawal was $1,000. He took it. It would be his last. Using Visa or debit would bring visibility to his whereabouts. He would catch a ride further west tonight. Pay cash, fake a name, and be gone.

"Downtown somewhere," he directed a taxi driver moments later. He turned in the backseat and watched through the rear window. There was no sign of either Sarah or Darryl. His absence would go unnoticed for another five maybe ten minutes, and then they'd be looking for him.

Elation flowed over him like the relief that follows a lanced blister. Obligation drained away in the backseat of that Chicago taxi. He could do anything he wanted. No more 4:20 a.m. alarm buzzers. No more requisite business meetings. He wouldn't have to be anywhere or do anything. Freedom was his to relish.

"Any place in particular, chief?" the driver asked.

"A good sports bar?" Jason wondered out loud. But before the balding driver had time to answer, he knew where to go. "Take me to the Sports Grill."

He remembered the bar's relaxed atmosphere from a previous trip. The beer was good too. Exactly what he needed.

Again, he glanced through the rear window. No one was following. He felt like a kid skipping school.

Do you know what you're doing?

This was not something the Jason he was used to did. At that moment, he came very close to calling it off.

The walls of protocol he'd let imprison him were crumbling. He would become a *new* person with a *new* life—disappearing from one and reappearing in another. As they drove across the city, he watched gray cement walls transition to rusting steel girders. Expensive shops to derelict buildings. Fancy suits to dirty, worn-out coats. Buildings of glass to tenements of windows.

They crossed a bridge.

It seemed he'd been trying to cross a bridge his whole life. Memories flashed through his head. At fifteen, he played hockey five nights a week on route to the NHL. At eighteen, he missed the draft and his ticket to the show. At nineteen, he was going to university. God had given him a brain. Math and science, his so called saviors.

By most accounts, he'd done well, yet he detested what he'd become. After graduating with a degree in business commerce, he swore he would make his mark and not succumb to his father's corporate world of drudgery and routine. That man had bowed to a boss his whole life. He vowed he would never submit to such an environment.

Denise was three months pregnant on their wedding day, having done all the other things he'd sworn he wouldn't. They were a family before they were a couple. He became his father. Maybe all sons did. Maybe it was inevitable. If the boss said jump, he was in the air and asking how high. He was a product of formal education, owned and driven by his employer. He was not naïve to what he'd become, having desecrated himself to a paycheck for a daily routine of going nowhere, in return for a burdensome mortgage and two leased cars in the driveway; he was a success. That success came from having. Not from any sort of personal fulfillment in his life. The gourmet kitchen, the ceramic tiles, the home theatre were there, all on payments, all trophies to his achievements.

He had forsaken his youth-minded enthusiasm for salaried mediocrity and—worst of all—knew it. He'd recognized when it started and made an attempt to change things. He'd started writing. Every morning, like clockwork—education had taught him that— he would get up at five and write for an hour before work. He was happy and thrived until the rejections toppled that dream too. It's remnants in the carton in his closet. Given another chance, could he be someone else, somewhere else?

Hell yeah. He was tired of fitting in. Tired of being someone he wasn't—tired of being tired. He would reinvent his life—his way. Maybe start by retelling his story, write the story his way. Like before, but catch a break this time.

He'd start by changing his name.

"Here y'are, sir. Thirty-two fifty."

Jason pulled two twenties out of his wallet.

"I'll need a receipt," he said.

"Sure," replied the driver.

Jason grabbed the strap of his laptop bag and realized what he'd asked for. His new program didn't require a receipt.

"Forget it," he said. "Who's your favorite movie star?"

The driver thought for a minute and then replied, "Sean Penn. Why?"

"No reason. Thanks."

Jason closed the door and stood on the sidewalk as the taxi drove away. He looked up at the sky where Sarah and Darryl would soon be sitting.

"Sean," he said to himself. "Not bad."

He paused and looked across the street, slinging the strap of his bag onto his shoulder.

"Yesssss!"

He clenched his hand in a fist pump.

The Sports Grill was slow in the midafternoon. The place was empty outside of a silver-haired man in a wrinkled, gray suit sitting at the bar. Jason pulled up a barstool at the other end and set his bag on the stool next to him.

"Afternoon," said a lively, female voice from behind the counter. "What can I get you?"

"Well ... let me think," he stammered, taken off guard by the flash of the young woman's green eyes. She was cute, probably a college student making ends meet. "What do you have on tap?"

"Just about anything you can think of." She smiled back. The reflection of the interior lights twinkled in her eyes as she wiped the polished countertop in front of him.

Spunky. He liked that. He imagined touching her young, tanned skin. Her breasts would be firm and deliciously soft and smooth.

"How about a pint of Sam Adams dark," he replied, registering Sting's "Be Still My Beating Heart" in the background.

"Coming right up!"

He loosened his tie and undid the top button of his dress shirt. Funny, he'd come all this way without undoing his tie. He put his elbows on the bar and inhaled his new freedom. He did not frequent places like this in the afternoon. This was cool, very cool.

"Ya here on biznuz?"

"I came down on business, yes," Jason replied.

The woman had been sitting one stool over from him for almost half an hour. Other than a few glances, she'd paid him little attention. The crimson lipstick she wore made her lips look like an open gash in her face. Her silk blouse was loose and unbuttoned to be obvious. Her skirt was slit at the front, and her crossed legs revealed the tips of blue spider veins on her thigh. Made up to be attractive, she had the reverse effect on Jason.

"Are ya stayin' for the weekend, darlin'?"

"Looks like it."

He couldn't tell whether her words were slurred from a speech impediment or alcohol consumption. He concluded the latter.

"Change of plans, huh?"

"You could say that."

"Where ya from?" she asked, becoming friendlier, turning to direct her legs toward him. She looked like a worn-out Cadillac with a smudged coat of polish to hide the rust on the fenders.

"Toronto," he replied without embellishment.

"I'm Jane," she offered.

"Sean," he replied with a slight smile.

"First time in Chicago, Sean?"

"No. Been a few times," he said, thinking to add, "for treatments."

"Oh really." Her expression changed as her interest faded. "Well, I hope you're okay."

She glanced at her wrist. There was no watch. "I'm s'pose to meet someone. Guess they're not showin'. I better go."

She gathered her things and left.

Satisfied, he took a sip of his third beer. Jane was not in the picture he saw for himself.

He looked around, noticing the bar had filled up. He felt more alone than when he'd had the place to himself.

His thoughts turned to Denise. The night before last had been a blowout. Months had passed since they'd made love. They had gone for long stretches before, but this time was crazy. It was sex now, not love. She didn't like him touching her and withdrew from his advances. Even a kiss could turn her head. Her hands would come up in front of her chest to avoid a hug. It drove him nuts. She said she didn't understand it. Said she was sorry. It was her, not him. The argument ended with her telling him he needed a different wife. She grabbed her pillow and left the bedroom.

Frustrated in his inability to resolve the issue, he had lain awake, imagining all kinds of scenarios. In the past, he had confronted her. *Was there someone else?* It had infuriated her that he would question her fidelity. *Had she been abused as a child?* No. *Did she trust him?* Yes. *Did she think it would change?* Maybe. *Was there any hope, any at all?* The answer was always the same. "I don't know, but I know I love you."

He loved her too, and there lied the rub. Maybe he was the one with the problem. You had to love yourself before you could love someone else, right? Could his failures as he saw them be the culprit? Maybe. Or could it be the dynamics kids brought into the mix? He wouldn't change that for the world. There were so many maybes. More than once he had speculated … if he could only start over again.

These misgivings swirled in his head as he sat at the bar. Now he could start over. Now he would … and then it hit him—like walking into a transparent wall of glass solid enough to drop him in his tracks. It was Jack and Lynn's smiling faces running to greet him as he came through the front door, screaming, "Daddy! Daddy!" Jack, older by two years with his arms wrapped around his waist, and Lynn with her small arms clenched around his knee, trying as best she could to stand on his foot with her three-year-old legs. Their eyes lit up in the excitement of seeing their daddy come home.

His sight blurred with tears. Was his life really that bad, making this worth not seeing and holding the two of them again? Was making this fantasy come true really worth that sacrifice? He stood up. He'd already missed his flight. He could catch a later one. Life was about balance; suffering was part of that balance. He sat back down. *Let's think about this, Jason.* If life didn't kill you, it made you stronger. Right?

Soon there were too many people and too many conversations surrounding him. Unaccustomed to the amount of alcohol he'd consumed only muddled his thoughts further. He needed air and some quiet time. Lost in the twist of sudden freedom, he felt imprisoned by his own indecision. He had the power to control his choice, but the responsibility of that choice was weighing him down. Could he live with it for the rest of his life? His only counsel—likely the least helpful source of all—was himself.

"What can I get you, hun?" a voice said, interrupting his thoughts.

He turned to find a middle-aged waitress standing in front of the table he'd moved to. She wore a black, short-sleeved blouse and black slacks. On the heavy side, her ample chest pulled hard on the silver buttons that held the front together. He got an eyeful when she leaned over to wipe his table. Averting his eyes from her freckled cleavage, he looked into her made-up face.

She smiled.

"Ah … a cheeseburger and fries will work," he stammered, self-conscious of where his eyes had been, "and a large draft."

The array of directions his life could take skewed his thinking and set his stomach churning. He knew what to do, yet didn't. Emotions interfered with his ability to decide. Feeling free for the first time in he couldn't remember how long, the responsibility of his decision brought on more discomfort. It made him second-guess what he was doing. Could he live with saying good-bye to the life he'd worked so hard, and sacrificed so much, to create?

The waitress brought his food and beer and set it down in front of him.

"Anything else I can get you?" she asked.

"Thanks," he said. His eyes flashed past her chest and up to her face. Her mouth was small, but her teeth were bleach-white and straight. Soft, blue eyes met his.

"Would you join me for a toast?" he asked, surprising himself by raising his glass with a smile. The alcohol was talking. "I know it likely breaks protocol … but the occasion warrants it. It would be a privilege … to have you join me."

He appeared to catch her off guard, which seemed odd for a waitress with her apparent experience. There was noticeable hesitation in her reply.

"Well, I …," she started to say, sliding the drink tray onto the table and placing a hand on her hip. "We're not supposed to consort with the clientele."

"Oh, but this is a client request. Isn't the customer always … right?"

It was her turn to call his play.

"My shift ends at eleven. Can you wait?"

Startled, he looked at his watch and forgot the toast to freedom he was about to make. *Was this really what he wanted?* The time was his now. He had nothing but time.

"Well," he replied, hesitating, and tipped his glass to her, ignoring her question. "Here's to freedom."

"We interrupt this broadcast to bring you a special report," announced a serious male voice over the Black Hawk game on the screen behind her. Jason set his glass back on the table. What world spectacle was coinciding with his? An instant later, a blonde news correspondent stood in front of a scene of chaos. Grave concern marked her pretty face but didn't affect the delivery of her report—smooth, clear, and precise. Jason let go of his beer upon hearing the words "air disaster."

"Two eyewitnesses say the jet split in half."

The picture switched to an on-the-scene camera where a haggard and horrified person spewed emotion. "I saw a flash and something fall off the plane." Another person standing nearby added, "The plane seemed to stumble … stall … then literally dropped."

"Air Canada flight 532 on route from Chicago to Toronto …," continued the correspondent.

His head went numb. External sound shut down. His hands went into their own action. He reached for his bag and knocked it off the chair beside him. He reached down and pulled it onto his lap. He fumbled with the zipper. He grabbed at a binder, his scheduler, a file folder. His hands shook in their haste. Where was it? A side pocket held the white pamphlet he was after. He didn't need to check. He knew the number. By some twist of fate, he hoped he was wrong.

The white pamphlet went on the table. He put his hand on top of it as if to prevent it from blowing away. Then, unaware of what he was doing, he replaced what had fallen from his bag and zipped it closed. Not once did he look at the ticket on the table.

"Something wrong?" his waitress asked.

"Wrong …" he answered in a voice disconnected from his body. It jarred him from his stupor. His hand returned to the pamphlet on the table.

"There's been no official statement from the airline as to the cause of the accident. We will provide you with …" the television correspondent continued on.

"What's the number on this ticket?" he asked, indicating the pamphlet with his eyes while pushing it toward her. For the first time, he noticed the woman's nametag—Leanne.

Her movements took on his hesitance.

"Where is … oh, here it is. A-C-5-3-2," she read without faltering, and turned to the television. He watched as she pointed with the ticket still in her hand. "Gives you second thoughts, doesn't it? Those poor …"

His face was ashen. He gripped the edge of the table.

"Are you all right?" she asked while at the same moment realizing what was in her hand. "Oh … my … God!" Leanne said, still holding the ticket he'd handed her. "You were … booked …"

People turned. A cell phone appeared in his hand. He didn't carry one. Leanne became flustered. Jason thumbed the number like he did when he used Denise's phone. Upon pressing the last number, he stopped.

Why was he calling? He *was* free. That was why he was here and not on the flight. His escape was now assured. He was being handed his freedom. The call would make it all for naught.

The noise of the bar returned to his ears. The surroundings flooded his head. There were so many voices, yet he felt so alone.

He'd left the airport with his decision and a sense of release. But the feeling of release had ended. Sarah and Darryl were gone. He was too technically—disappearance *fait accompli*. Yet it didn't seem so important anymore. His life was but the push of a button away. Yet being dead didn't sit well with him. For reasons that now defied explanation, he wanted to tell Denise he was alive. He needed her to hear his voice. He wanted to be alive. He wanted his life.

His grip tightened on the cell phone as if trying to squeeze counsel from its electronics. His thumb pressed the green button.

The phone rang. He counted four rings before the line connected.

"Hello," Denise answered. Her voice was weak, wretched, as if sadness would be an improvement on how she felt.

He listened to the static crackle on the line.

"Honey," was all he could manage before his voice cracked and disappeared. He couldn't even whisper. Their kitchen radio was playing in the background.

He tried again.

"Denise, it's me."

There was no response, only the sound of the radio—a reporter describing the disaster.

"Jason?" Denise's voice changed, soft and comforting as only she could speak. It was the sound of hope.

"Yes. It's me."

He wanted to hold her in his arms, to hug her tightly. Feel her realness, her warm skin against his. "I'm okay."

Leanne looked at him, smiling. Tears glistened on her cheeks.

"Oh my god!" Denise cried, her voice growing louder with relief and disbelief. "But your plane, your flight. I'm listening ... the radio ... and the crash. How is it possible? It's not possible ..."

"I know, Denise," he started. "It doesn't make any sense. Thank God I missed my flight. I'm still in Chicago." He was never able to explain why he hadn't got on the flight.

Denise kept talking. She was beyond relief. Tears would be running down her cheeks as they were his. Her eye shadow would be smudged. Her happiness mimicked his.

⸻◈⸻

Jason spent many years trying to rationalize what had happened. Why had he been saved from the crash? *God?*

On his return home, he wasn't back a week before he began pulling his stories out of the box in the closet. He'd been spared for a reason. Though the stories had been written in another place and time, they were his. He'd created them. They renewed him. He found solace in editing and rewriting. It wasn't long before he didn't have room—or desire—for his job. They sold the house and one of the cars. Six months later, he sold his first story to a small magazine on the East Coast. Their savings were gone, and money was thin, but he was living—in fact, thriving.

For some time, he struggled with losing Sarah and Darryl and how their tragedy changed his life. He'd had difficulty calling them friends when they worked together, being their boss and older, but that ceased to matter. They were his friends whatever the case. He missed them.

More importantly, what he came to realize was his want to disappear wasn't about Denise at all, but his life. Life was hard. Having bought into the façade, the tedium, and the measures of success, his contempt for his own inability to change had degenerated into his need to try and flee from himself.

He never realized how much he had to change to become who he really was.

Mile Twenty-Eight

Both his hands were on the steering wheel. The morning light had replaced the need for his headlamps. But Tom wasn't thinking about his lights. The woman he'd left was fighting for her life. He didn't know her name. Freedom was gone for the kid in the cruiser. The more this mix of thoughts stirred in his head, the clearer things became. Through their disorder, order was taking place.

He raised his coffee cup. It was empty. He brought it to his lips anyway.

Work would be different today.

Most prominent in his mind wasn't what he'd just gone through. Strangely it was those he worked with. Most were likeable and smart and educated. They could reason and solve problems. Most followed the rules and did their work well. But there was something else. No one seemed to care much about whether what they worked on was connected or why it was or wasn't important. Most knew and did their jobs well, but that was it. And that was the point. They were doing their jobs—blank and nondescript, being objective as they'd been taught with little or no feeling or connection. Their hearts, their beating hearts, their passion and emotion were missing or locked out. They weren't living in concert with what they were doing. There was fuzziness to their conviction—that living connection. Most were concerned about how they were measured and whether what they worked on was in process or on schedule or met whatever technical requirements were deemed necessary for the project. Not whether it fit together or connected or was in any way meaningful or valuable to anyone—even themselves. Or whether they loved or even liked what they were doing. They knew how the product worked and sometimes the technology behind it, like they'd learned to study for the right answer to an exam question. But that didn't connect the dots for what was unseen when all wasn't apparent and obvious. Moreover, without connecting the dots, the result—the product or now the project—was more often than not useless or of little value to anyone, no matter how many times they were told how good it was. Value didn't have to be quantified or even understood; it just had to be there. Value connected everything with people.

What was the so-called "new" interface they were working on going to do for anyone that it wasn't doing now? What would new symbols do other than confuse those who used the current ones? What did a new box with rounded corners do for anyone? Tom didn't like his answers. If he couldn't understand their value how the hell was anybody else going to? Value was elusive at the best of times but someone had to like or find a use for the product—no matter what it was. Few in the company seemed to grasp or even care that it mattered.

Tom's thoughts moved to his story. He'd given into rejection too many times but had refused to admit it. Deep down there had to be another way to make what he wanted work. The glue to that something in his life that brought meaning and purpose had all but dissipated. "Lost his way" some might say, but he wasn't looking for what to call it. He could feel it. He could no longer stand living to measures that were not his own. Not living up to who he was or who he could be was the real culprit behind his current predicament. Why he was even thinking of a secret rendezvous with Silke was stupidity at a very high level. He needed to escape, but escape that hurt Janet— whom he loved dearly—or Jill and Lacey? Not living up to who he was had festered inside him for a long time. It had grown into an evil cancer of misery and despair and inappropriate action. The so-called Plan B looked more attractive because it was. It was supposed to. When things got tough, it was always easier to give in. But the pain of giving in rankled and never went away. And the cost—that devastating, unmeasured price that was paid—was fractured families and damaged loved ones that he saw all around him every day. In the news, in the office, in the neighborhood, recovery was spoken of with delight, but the hurt never went away. Did he really want to be in that boat? Because the same boat was closing in to pick him up too, if he hadn't already climbed aboard. He didn't need to live that way, but he was way down the road of allowing others' measures to dictate his. He saw it now like never before. Like him, they were scared cowards. Doing everything in their power not to be revealed in order to show in some way that they were successful. It was a human need in the desperate pursuit for meaning and purpose—if not survival.

It wasn't Janet he didn't love anymore. Who he hated, what disgusted him most—was what he'd allowed himself to become. He'd let himself down long ago. He'd given into doing things he detested. To have things he didn't want. To show people he didn't even like. So he could look successful. He was making it all right. All at the expense of everything he really cared about.

How could it be so backward? How did it get so fucked up?

Silke was a way to keep him a float. She was hope, curiosity, and fantasy all built into one: all a part of the means without an end—as fucked as that could be.

Tom pulled into the company parking lot. He found a space near the back. Unusual, as his routine was to park close to the front. Come early. Keep the walk short and efficient. But he wasn't early today. Circumstances had prevented that.

He opened the car door as a gust of wind blew past him. Yesterday, he would have cursed the "fucking" wind.

He stood alone in the parking lot. The other cars were parked in neat rows. He opened the rear driver's side door. Something turned in his stomach. Heat rose up his back and around his neck. His face seemed to close as his eyes filled. He grabbed the doorframe as his stomach tightened. Tears rolled down his cheeks. For a few seconds, he couldn't stop. Then a smile hinted on his lips.

His laptop bag sat on the seat in its customary place for his drive in. He didn't move to retrieve it but instead closed the door.

His prototype car worked. His plan was solid. There had to be a way—but it wouldn't be here. More would come—but not at this place. He didn't know how, but he would find a way. Love was like that.

He smiled—a real smile. One he hadn't felt in a long time. He wiped his face with his palms.

He knew what he had to do. It'd been a week since he'd run his driverless prototype on the basement floor, but only a few days since he'd rewritten the business plan to present to the board. A business plan they would never see. He was itching to get going even in the short space of time since making his decision—somewhere between the old, redbrick house and where he was now standing. He couldn't shut it down anymore. His train was leaving the station. He couldn't stop it. Like eating, he could stop for a while, but he would have to eat again. Driverlessness had made him crazy. He wouldn't and couldn't be happy until he made a go of it. It was his future—*the* future. Something beyond him had chosen. It was no longer in him to let it go. He had to relent or that same force would ruin all that was good in his life. The decision, as it turned out, was quite easy.

At eight fifteen that day, after his drive in, Tom Johnson ended his journey as an employee.

It was his time.